THE

EXHIBITION

OF

Female Flagellants

http://www.birchgrovepress.com

ISBN:
978-0-9871953-2-6

Birchgrove Press brings together in one volume two texts representing the developing corpus of late eighteenth- and early nineteenth-century English sexual fiction focusing on flagellation: *Exhibition of Female Flagellants* and *Part the Second of the Exhibition of Female Flagellants*. Comprising collections of anecdotes about the pleasures of flogging, these novellas focus on birching in aristocratic domestic and scholastic contexts, emphasise the display of blood, and extol the aphrodisiacal qualities of flowers. The author or authors are not known.

Part one, *Exhibition of Female Flagellants* was first published c. 1780. The title page of the earliest known edition (undated) states it was printed for George Peacock but this name may be false. Erotica publishers often provided false or misleading details in an effort to confound prosecuting authorities. *Exhibition of Female Flagellants* was reprinted by George Cannon c. 1830 as *The Exhibition of Female Flagellants* and by William Dugdale c. 1860. Part two, *Part the Second of the Exhibition of Female Flagellants*, was first published about 1785, probably also by George Peacock. It was reprinted by Dugdale c. 1866. John Camden Hotten reprinted both volumes in 1872. He added the publication date 1777, which is conceivable, to volume one.

This Birchgrove Press edition of *Exhibition of Female Flagellants* and its sequel is based on Hotten's reprints. The image of Miss Mary Wilson wielding a birch graced Cannon's edition; the latter was 'Printed at the Expense of THERESA BERKLEY, for the Benefit of Mary Wilson'. (See Pisanus Fraxi [Henry Spencer Ashbee], *Index Librorum Prohibitorum*, 1877: 244 and 345; Ashbee attributes the Cannon edition to 'JOHN CANNON'. Ashbee's bibliographic record for both books is reprinted in the Appendix.)

Mary Wilson is one of English flagellant literature's greatest heroines: her name appears frequently in flagellant fiction as an author, publisher, and translator. It may have been the pseudonym of Erasmus Perkins, who was producing books on birch discipline in the late 1820s (to confound matters, Perkins' name may be one of Cannon's aliases), but it also appears to have been used as a literary in-joke that many readers would have recognized and enjoyed.

Miss Mary Wilson

THE

EXHIBITION

OF

Female Flagellants

Parts One and Two

BIRCHGROVE PRESS
MMXII

CONTENTS

Part One

EXHIBITION

OF

FEMALE FLAGELLANTS

IN THE

Modest and Incontinent World.

Proving from Indubitable FACTS,

That a Number of LADIES take a SECRET PLEASURE,

In WHIPPING their own,

AND CHILDREN COMMITTED TO THEIR CARE;

AND THAT THEIR PASSION

FOR EXERCISING AND FEELING THE

PLEASURE OF A BIRCH-ROD,

FROM OBJECTS OF THEIR CHOICE,

OF BOTH SEXES,

IS TO THE FULL AS PREDOMINANT,

AS THAT OF MANKIND.

Now First Publifhed,

From Authentic Anecdotes, French and English, found in a Lady's Cabinet.

LONDON:

Printed for G. Peacock, No. 66 Drury Lane.

MDCCLXXVII

EXHIBITION

OF

Female Flagellants, &c.

MERE fiction (says Clarissa, closing the Fashionable Lectures, which she had been just reading), ridiculous nonsense! — What, my dear? said Flirtilla, turning round from her toilet. Is it possible, my dear, said the first lady, that men delight in being whipped by women? Very true, indeed, said Flirtilla; and what you may think as extraordinary, many of your own sex take as great delight in whipping children; and when they are not in the way they make each other feel the tingling pleasures of a birch rod.

If you doubt my assertion, I will bring you proof positive — and the very lady will be of our tea-party this evening. If you should not credit her testimony, my assertion shall be strengthened by that of two ladies — old practitioners in this mode of pleasure. This passion, or whim, in woman, is of older birth than you can imagine; and as the fair hand and arm of a lady is a principal object in the scene, I shall turn to Mrs. Behn's glowing description of one of her favourite ladies:— "The beautiful colour and proportion of your arm is inimitable, and your hand is dazzling, fine, small, and plump! long-pointed fingers delicately turned; dimpled on the snowy outside, but adorned within with rose, all over the soft palm. O, *Iris!* nothing equals your fair hand — that hand, of which Love so often makes such use to draw his bow, when he would send the arrow home with more success; and which irresistibly wounds those, who possibly have not yet seen your eyes: and when you have been veiled, that lovely hand has gained you a thousand adorers! and I have heard Damon say, without the aid of more beauties, that alone had been sufficient to have made an absolute conquest o'er his soul. And he has often vowed it never touched him but it made his blood run with little irregular motions in his veins, his breath beat short and double, his blushes rise, and his very soul dance!"

There, my dear! there's a charming description for you! What magic in every sentence! What genius could soar beyond it? Is there a heart existing but would bound with rapture on seeing such a hand exercise a rod? Bless me, said Clarissa, you talk as if you were as fond of the sport as the most enthusiastic of them. I confess it freely, said Flirtilla, I am fond of it to excess, when the object inflames my blood and administers it with irresistible grace! Grace! grace! said Clarissa; I protest I cannot comprehend your meaning. Know, then, thou silly girl, there is a manner in handling this sceptre of felicity that few ladies are happy in: it is not the impassioned and awkward brandish of a vulgar female that can charm, but the deliberate and elegant manner of a woman of rank and fashion, who displays all that dignity in every action, even to the flirting of her fan, that leaves an indelible wound. What a difference between high and low life in this particular! To see a vulgar woman, when provoked by her children, seize them as a tyger would a lamb, rudely expose their posteriors, and correct them with an open hand, or rod more like a broom that a neat collection of twigs elegantly tied together; while a well-bred lady coolly and deliberately brings her child or pupil to task; and when in error, so as to deserve punishment, commands the incorrigible Miss to bring her the rod, go on her knees, and beg, with uplifted hands, an excellent whipping; which ceremony gone through, she commands her to lye across her lap, or to mount on her maid's shoulders; and then, with the loveliest hands imaginable, removes every impediment from the whimpering lady's b——e; who, all the time, with tears and entreaties of the sweetest kind, implores her dear mother or governess to pardon her; all which the lovely disciplinarian listens to with the utmost delight — running over with rapture, at the same time, those white angelic orbs, that in a few minutes she crimsons as deep as the finest rose, with a well-exercised and elegantly-handled rod!

Miss B—ge—n, a corpulent but handsome woman, with whom I passed many pleasant hours at Bristol Hot Wells, was passionately fond of this exercise. Her story has somewhat very singular in it.

She had been addressed, under the age of five-and-twenty, by an officer of Cavalry, who, when he brought matters to a closure, boasted of favours she had granted him, of such a complexion, that she renounced him and all his sex for ever. No woman can hold the monster, man, in greater abhorrence, and she has the most singular mode of retaliating upon the sex you have ever heard of. It made me stare with astonishment.

Sitting with her one evening, a smart youth, her nephew, between twelve and fourteen years old, and too big, as I imagined, for chastisement from a woman, entered the room crying, with a complaint against his sister, who was a great favourite with the lady: she brought them face to face, and it clearly appeared he was the aggressor. Miss B. dismissed the young lady, and rising from her chair, she brought a rod from a drawer, and, with the utmost coolness, commanded him to strip. The boy, well acquainted, we may suppose, with her temper, used no entreaties for pardon, and though I imagined he could, from his size, get the better of her in a struggle, yet he never used any, but with seeming pleasure unbuttoned his breeches; and, walking undaunted up to her, she pulled them down to his heels, and instantly stretched him along the sopha, where she whipped him with a severity I had never seen before; and what amazed me was, the boy would not acknowledge himself in error to the last; and arose with more pleasure in his countenance than anguish.

As soon as he had gone out of the room, I told her my surprise at his intrepidity; and she assured me *she* could never get a tear from him, though he had been severely whipped once or twice by his schoolmaster, and cried even on his return home. Depend upon it, said I, this boy is fond of being whipped by a woman. She said she could not think so, for she had whipped him with such severity at all times, that it must have given him more pain than pleasure. Why, yes, replied I, from your manner of exercising the rod, I am convinced you whip with severity; and I think, at the same time, you take a particular pleasure in this business.

I have been now used to it for some years, said she; and what will surprise you, my dear girl, I got such applause from a lady not long ago, who had been present at a similar scene, that as soon as the boy left the room, she embraced me, and pressing my hand with transport, begged I would suffer her to represent my niece.

I could not conceive what she was at till she dropped on her knees, implored, with streaming eyes (for she absolutely cried), forgiveness from her dear aunt for insulting her, and declaring she would never offend me again. All the time she was on her knees she was kissing my hand with greater ecstasy than it had ever been kissed before. Still I thought she imitated the child, and was in jest, till she — finding me tardy, or rather, ignorant of her meaning — bounced away to the table where I had placed the rod, and, putting it into my hand, begged forgiveness in the same lunatic manner.

She had gone too far now for me to be ignorant any longer of her meaning; so I instantly got up, put on an air of authority and passion; raised her clothes above her waist; and, having stretched her along the sopha, I made her caper under the rod for full ten minutes, with short intermissions, and arose from her frequently seizing hold of the rod, kissing my hand, looking up to me with tears, begging earnestly forgiveness, and every other extravagance that children use in the same situation.

As soon as she was done, and when I thought she had recovered her senses, I importuned her to tell me the first rise of such an extraordinary whim.

She told me she was placed under the tuition of a beautiful French Governess a short while after her arrival from the West Indies (for she was a Creole), and this Gallic lady frequently exercised the rod on her, but in such a manner that she absolutely grew fond of it; and ere she had been her pupil one year, they administered it almost every day on both sides; and she could never see a woman of elegance, with a hand and arm she liked, without wishing and seeking the pleasure from her.

Upon my honour, Miss B, said I, you must then have been one of her first favourites, for you are not only blessed with one of the most bewitching persons, and the sweetest expression of feature, but you may challenge the female world, and come off the victor, in exhibiting your snowy hand and arm, and the plump beauties of your bosom!

Do you really think so, my dear? said she, with a magic smile, looking at her hand, and turning a beautiful brilliant ring which she then wore.

To convince you I am serious, I will esteem it a particular favour to taste the same felicity from your hand this moment.

Heavens! my dear, you jest.

No, upon my honour, I do not; and to convince you I am serious, I will go into the next room — from which place you must bring me to the sopha (finding me idling there), and use me as you did your nephew just now.

And were you mad enough, said Clarissa, to go through this torture?

Rapture! Rapture! my sweet girl — call it by no other

term. The moment I saw her enter the room, where she caught me romping by myself, and felt her soft angelic hand catch hold of my arm to bring me to the sopha, my blood mantled within me as if I had been in a fever: but there was another charm about her that enraptured me, which was her dress: for dress certainly heightens this pleasure with both sexes. This evening we were both engaged to go to a ball, and she had dressed herself in a very elegant manner. To be brief, my dear girl, I was whipped by this lovely woman, not only then, but several times since, in such a charming manner, that I shall never think of her but with the utmost delight; and there is not a lady who was afterwards of our society, or whipping academy, but was delighted with her manner; and she herself, before she had whipped me a third time, took a liking to the sport from my hands, and was as much in love with it.

She had the prettiest manner of tying a rod, and selected the nicest twigs that ever you saw. And now that I recollect, I protest I can shew you one of them she gave me to remember her, the very last time I had the happiness of being in her company.

Here it is, said Flirtilla, tied, by her own magic hand,

with a pink ribbon; and now, that I am in the humour, you shall exercise it on me!

You are a fine showy girl; and I think this lovely hand of yours would do honour to the rod! Come, my dear Clarissa, don't refuse me.

I am afraid I shall be a bungler, said the blushing charmer; I never whipped any one in my life.

Come, then, said Flirtilla, you shall turn up; and from the specimen you taste from my hands, you will know how to act.

O fie! said Clarissa, upon my honour you shall not lift my clothes — indeed, said the fair one struggling, you shall not. — For Heaven's sake, Flirtilla, let me alone! I won't be whipped, upon my honour.

Then you must prove yourself the stronger of the two, said Flirtilla, who had by this time not only carried her into her bed-chamber, but had her stretched upon the bed.

Upon my honour, said Flirtilla, I'll only tickle you as if you were a child — so keep your legs still till I raise your petticoats.

You shan't raise them! said Clarissa, plunging. I will raise them, said Flirtilla, I am resolved; and with a little more struggling, the whole prospect was as much in view as Eve's in the garden of Eden. You see, said Flirtilla, I am as good as my word, and your pretty a—e shall feel, too, what a step-mother can do to a bold girl! yes, my pretty Miss, you shall, I am determined. Flirtilla exercised the rod, with some pauses and admonitions, for a full quarter of an hour, which Clarissa bore with seeming pleasure; and rose to take it in hand perfectly well pleased.

She instantly, by desire, assumed the character of Flirtilla's Governess, and having stretched her, with some seeming reluctant struggles on the part of Flirtilla, on the bed, she uncovered to the waist the plumpest, fairest, and most beautiful posteriors that ever charmed mankind. Clarissa herself stood entranced at the lovely view, and suspended the rod, till Flirtilla, impatient for the delightful combat, cried out like a terrified child, O, my dear, lovely Governess, forgive me! Don't whip me this time, pray don't! you'll find me an excellent girl in future; and I'll never deserve a whipping from your lovely hand! Indeed, I won't. — In this manner she continued to implore forgiveness, kicking and plunging the whole time, till Clarissa was almost weary tickling her with the rod.

She then got up, embraced her, and vowed she would not rest till she introduced her to her whipping intimates, as she had proved herself an excellent disciplinarian with the rod.

That evening, said Clarissa (from whose manuscripts and conversation these anecdotes are collected), Flirtilla introduced me to Lady Caroline, who received me with every mark of high-breeding, and insisted on my supping with her. There were but four of her tea-party remained to supper — viz., Flirtilla, Lady Caroline, Mademoiselle Boc——e, and myself.

We had not been half-an-hour by ourselves, when Flirtilla, with an archness peculiar to herself, introduced me to Lady Caroline as her step-daughter just arrived from a boarding-school; and, looking significantly at Ma'emoiselle, You are in future, said she, my dear woman, to superintend and finish her education. I have had her under my care some time, and assure you she is an excellent girl, particularly after a good whipping, which I have given her sometimes. — My dear Lady Caroline, I hope you will excuse me. She is now under your dominion: I have complied with your request in bringing her home, and I doubt not but the young lady will find a tender and an affectionate step-mother in you. I shall treat her according to her deserts, I assure, said Lady Caroline. I have held it an unpardonable crime, when a girl deserves chastisement, to withhold the rod; and I assure you, upon my honour, it gives me particular pleasure to exercise it on unruly boys and girls. I am to the full as fond of whipping bold children as the lovely Mrs. E——.

She has a most bewitching manner indeed, said Ma'emoiselle, and I know none but your ladyship that excels her.

Pardon me, my lovely woman, said Lady Caroline, *you* leave all our sex at a considerable distance when you have an object you admire under correction. How have I seen my little brother, your pupil, whom you confess to be passionately fond of whipping, gaze on you with rapture, during the many struggles you have had, letting down his trousers! Who could behold unmoved the brilliancy of your eyes, the lovely cast of your features, the fall of your shoulders and the rising of your bosom, elegant as a Grecian Venus! You remember my compliment when you first charmed me with the rod in the character of a governess—

> All things around with beams of beauty shine
> And roses spring beneath your feet divine;
> What awful lustre lightens from your face!
> Which proves thee, charmer, of celestial race

Very pretty indeed, said Flirtilla, and admirably well applied. But, pray, who is this Mrs. E—— you mentioned just now; I never heard of her before?

Mrs. E—— was bred in a convent. Her parents were Roman Catholics, and having no daughter but her, they foolishly imagined a convent education far superior to any this country could boast. There she lived till she had gained her five-and-twentieth year, at which time her father died, and she found herself in possession of twenty-five thousand pounds. At the importunities of a fond mother, who went to see her once every year, she visited England, and being a girl of good fortune, it is not to be wondered at that she had a crowd of admirers. In her visits, she was very much taken with that part of a widower's family that in general is found most disagreeable, at least to young ladies, *his children*. She observed they were indulged in by a weak father in everything, and were consequently very disobedient and unruly. Upon this gentleman, though verging on forty, she fixed her affection, and being a woman of ungovernable spirit, she was happy to find him an easy pusillanimous creature. The match was scarcely mentioned when it was concluded on, and in a few days after, she found herself in the seat of empire in his house. She had six little subjects to govern, three of which were then at school in Herefordshire, which were instantly ordered home, as she said she would undertake to finish their education, which, indeed, was in her power, for she was a very sensible woman; but that was not her intent altogether. It was the boys that were ordered from school, who seemed very happy in leaving a place so irksome to youth in general; but they had only escaped a male for a female flagellator. As soon as she was married, she discharged all the servants, and hired a set of her own choosing; and among the rest, she took care to engage a French lady for her own woman, whose disposition she knew would just suit her.

Mrs. E—— was of the first order of beauty; had a noble person, fine turned limbs, good skin, fine blue eyes, as brilliant as Venus', and when not ruffled by passion, was certainly very captivating. If she but stepped across the room, she discovered uncommon dignity and elegance, and every motion expressed that *Jen ne scai quoi* an elegant French woman is so idolized for. In short, my dear, I never think of her without exclaiming with the Poet—

O, with what bloom, what flower of youth she shone!
How her cheeks blush'd a colour all her own—
A genuine red, like roses newly blown!
With her what woman could pretend to vie
A whiter forehead, or a lovelier eye?
Whose frame was like the world, an elegant soul
Spoke in each part, and sparkl'd thro' the whole;
Each limb did wanton Loves and Graces bear:
There lodg'd their arms, their bows and arrows there.

Though this whipping passion was inextinguishable within her, yet she was never observed to take the rod in hand without some offence to accession it. She was convinced where there was such a number of children, and they ungovernable, many bickerings would arise, which would give her an opportunity to amuse herself with the rod. The first that gave her occasion to handle the rod was a boy of seven years old, who was so stupid at a lesson she gave him, that she was resolved to try the effects of birch on his posteriors. Her French woman was ordered to bring an excellent rod, which she had no sooner done, than she proceeded to exercise it; but she found the boy too strong for her. The maid instantly whips off her garters, and, with the assistance of her mistress, ties his hands behind him; and then they found him manageable enough. They instantly unbuttoned his breeches, and let them down to his knees; and, having placed him across his mother's lap, and the woman holding his legs, his mother whipped him till the twigs flew about the room.

This was the first sample of her severity with the rod she gave since she was married; and it made such an impression on the rest of the children, that they trembled in her presence. A few hours after the boy was complaining, with tears, of her treatment to his eldest sister, who advised him to burn the rod the first opportunity. This was overheard by the maid, who informed her lady of the affair. The young lady was summoned to the parlour, where she denied the fact, was confronted by the maid, and horsed by her in an instant. The lady made as free with Miss's lovely b——e as with her brother's; and convinced her she met with a mother fond to excess of exercising the rod.

Wherever this lady visited she was called by the children the school-mistress, and they dreaded the sight of her.

In my visits, said Lady Caroline, I had heard much talk of this lady, and was so pleased with what I heard, that I soon got not only into her company, but formed a friendship that has continued to this day.

The first time I had the pleasure of beholding this lovely woman at the exercise we are so fond of was at her country-house, where I spent the happiest months of my life. A lovely girl, her step-daughter (whose beauties I firmly believe she envied), made her an impertinent answer as we three sat at work in the saloon. The mother did not say a sentence in reply, but instantly left the room, and returning in less than a minute, with a neat rod in her hand, she commanded Miss to lie across her lap, who instantly, with disdain pictured in her countenance, complied. I sat directly opposite the young lady's posterior prospect, and protest to you, upon my honour, when her mother lifted her clothes to the middle, and displayed the seat of beauty, I think I never beheld anything so lovely. She whipped her very smartly, and I affirm no eyes in the world could sparkle with more transport than the lady's during the whole of the punishment.

This observation led me to think this lovely woman *one of us* in the highest sense, and the instant Miss left the room, which was in a few minutes, I requested to know if I was right.

She denied it for some time, and blushed exceedingly. I am certain, said I, my dear creature, if I was one of your daughters, you would tell me another story, and I could read in your eyes during your whole proceeding with Maria what I assert. You are afraid to trust me with the secret, I plainly perceive, but I will trust you with as great a one on my part. Know then, thou angelic woman, said I, kissing her lovely hand, it would be my highest felicity to be whipped by you this moment!

Are your really serious? said she.

Do not procrastinate this bliss, for heaven's sake, my charming friend, but assume the character of my offended governante instantly.

To be brief, my dear girls, this beautiful woman that

moment confessed her passion, and I never was so enraptured as through the whole of her punishment, which she told me she would inflict pretty smartly, and every stroke of which convinced me of the truth of her assertion.

I remember she told me a remarkable story of a lady she was intimate with, who was an excellent hand at exercising a birch-rod.

The late Lord L——, when very young, was so pleased with the exercise of the rod, that he courted the felicity from the hands of his mother's maid repeatedly. This giddy girl happened to mention this circumstance to a baronet's lady (her late mistress), who was of so avaricious a disposition, that she instantly conceived a notion of adding something considerable to her purse, by taking proper notice of this secret.

Flush with the idea, she managed to have an interview with him that evening at her house, by sending for him to spend the evening with her daughter.

When he arrived he was surprised to find none of the family, above those of the kitchen, at home.

The youth was about this period twelve years old, and the lady about thirty. She was by no means handsome, yet she possessed those requisites whipping gentlemen and ladies idolize so highly. She was tall, and very lusty, had a quick black eye, a neat, plump, white hand and arm, and was in her nature as well as appearance as proud as any woman the lovers of birch would desire to exercise the rod.

He had not sat ten minutes when she handed him a book to read to her; it was Milton's Paradise Lost, which at that age he could read but so so. She took the book out of his hand, and looking full in his eyes with an air of austerity, told him if he was her son she would instantly let down his breeches and whip him well.

At that moment (as he expressed himself after to her) the blood boiled in his veins, and he felt himself in a blaze. She saw his situation, and taking him by the hand, asked him how he should like to be under her tuition? He replied in the negative. Come, come, said she, seating him on her lap, I know you would like it vastly, I can read it in your eyes! Confess now, you bold boy, would not you like to see me take the rod in hand, make you go upon your knees and beg a whipping, and then let me strip your breeches to your heels! Her manner of enforcing this confession was such, that she declared he instantly disclosed the secret. He frankly owned the whole, and she immediately conducted him to her dressing room.

When she got him in she locked the door: then made him bring a rod she had in readiness, which he put in her hand. She then held a long conversation with him on his knees, on his many crimes, and deliberately let down his breeches to his heels; she then laid him across her lap, and after removing his shirt above his waist, made use of all the tricks she had heard gentlemen were fond of who loved the rod, such as settling him on her knee, handling his b——e, at the same time pulling his breeches lower, tucking in his shirt, and talking of the ladies who spare the rod and spoil the child, bidding him at the same time prepare for something very delicious from her hand, for nothing was half so pleasing to her as exercising a rod on a bold boy's b——e. She then held him fast with one hand round the middle, and whipped him with the rod so severely that he was obliged to cry aloud. She gave him a dozen strokes every spell, then argued with him, and never remitted of the severity of her whipping the whole time, which was about a quarter of an hour.

It is an undoubted fact, that that woman who uses the

rod with most severity, keeps her culprits down, and every way treat them as tho' they were in fact bold children, not only gives the most pleasure, but makes such an impression, that they have the highest veneration for them; and ladies who have exercised the rod most, like a severe mother, governess, step-mother, &c., have retained their lovers as long as they have possessed any charms of face or person; while those, however beautiful, who are not as deep skilled in the mystery, never keep a lover for more than two or three whippings at most. This lady was deep in the secret, and she profited by it, for his lordship was very liberal to her to the day of his death.

I am certain, ladies, you agree in what I have advanced; I am not the only person that has made this declaration.

You are very right, my dear, said Ma'emoiselle; it is a very general observation, believe me; and, I am sure, all my pupils will bear testimony to my conduct in this.

I will, for one, upon my honour, said Lady Caroline; and I for another, said Flirtilla.

But, now I think of it, said Lady Caroline, turning to Flirtilla, and putting on an air of authority, pray, Miss, do you know this letter? (pulling one from her pocket). No, indeed, Ma'am, said Flirtilla, seemingly much embarrassed. Are you certain of it? said Lady Caroline, taking her by the hand and looking full in her eyes. Yes, upon my honour, my dear Mamma, said Flirtilla.

Well, said Mademoiselle, you are the most confident little baggage I ever knew. I found this seal in your own room, and it corresponds with the impression on the letter. You have been striving for some time to breed a quarrel between Miss Bloom—d and your Mamma; and you would have effected it if I had not been fortunate enough to secure this abusive letter this morning in your own room.

Very well, Miss, said Lady Caroline, rising from her chair with great *hauteur*, and leaving the room.

My dear Ma'emoiselle, said Flirtilla, dropping on her knees, pray get me pardoned this time, and I'll love you while I live.

No, said Ma'emoiselle, I will not interfere, I assure you; you deserve to be well whipped, and I hope she will not spare the rod. I wish she would deliver you over to my correction. I promise you I would make an excellent use of the rod.

At the expiration of about ten minutes, Lady Caroline entered with the instrument of pleasure in her hand. But it was not that that detained her for so long. Flirtilla, who idolized Lady Caroline's hand and arm, could not bear to see it hold the rod without the ornaments of pearls, bracelets, a wedding and diamond rings. Her bosom and neck were set off in the same manner; and her legs and feet, which were elegantly formed, were as beautifully embellished with the neatest silk shoes and brilliant buckles of the first fashion. But the following is the best picture of this bewitching woman:—

> Her front like marble smooth, like lilies white
> Fair Cynthia lustred o'er with silver light;
> Upon her cheeks *Aurora* Roses spread,
> And dy'd 'em in the Morning's brightest red!
> *Venus* the sweetly charming smile imprest,
> And her soft lips with balmy pleasures bless'd;
> While love, the god himself, o'er all the mass,
> Dancing delightful shew'd his heavenly face,
> Led on the laughing Joys, and every sister Grace.

Come, Miss, said Lady Caroline; come here to me this minute, till you and I settle accompts. It is some days since you tasted a rod from my hands; and, I remember, you then promised me would not deserve a whipping as long as you'd live. — Horse her this moment, Ma'emoiselle; and, I am sure, this good lady will take a particular pleasure in holding up the clothes of so bold a girl.

O, Mamma! O, Ma'emoiselle! my dear, Ma'emoiselle, don't horse me! Upon my honour, I'll be a good girl in future, said Flirtilla, repeatedly. Keep her up tight, Ma'emoiselle, said Lady Caroline; I have her exposed now to my wish, and she shall feel the rod pretty smartly.

By this time, said Clarissa, with my assistance, she had pinned the tail of her shift to her shoulders; and, having placed a low stool under her feet, that she might be no great burthen to Ma'emoiselle, she took the rod in hand.

What Flirtilla felt that moment might be read in her eyes, which sparkled with ecstasy! Her entreaties were of the tenderest kind; and the motion of her lovely alabaster prospect would have transported an anchoret to madness.

Lady Caroline was throughout the scene the most salacious woman I ever beheld.

Her manner of standing, and motions, were grace and dignity itself! The haughty manner of delivering her lecture, was such as I had not heard from Flirtilla; nor have not heard to this hour from any other woman.

How Flirtilla could bear the whipping amazed me, as Lady Caroline exercised the rod with such severity, that that prospect, which a few minutes before could emulate the lily, now excelled the rose.

Though after repeated frolics in this way with Flirtilla, I must confess I was pleased with it; yet I could not be reconciled to the severity I was a witness of from the hands of Lady Caroline; but I soon understood she carried her passion to greater lengths with others — particularly Ma'emoiselle B., who has been whipped by her till the blood has been near starting; and she would not condescend to whip any of her intimates unless they would suffer her to act as she thought proper.

A few days after we were invited to the country-seat of Lady Carmine, who is in possession of a greater fund of anecdote in this way than any lady living.

Among many very singular whims, she related the following, which from her own knowledge she affirmed was authentic.

As the account would be much better in her own words than any other, I shall give every particular in as concise and perfect a manner as my memory can dictate.

I had the honour, said Lady Carmine, with many ladies now in this country, to be particularly noticed in Paris, some years ago, by the Duchess of ———.* This lady, then verging on forty, carried this whipping whim to very unlimited lengths.

She had a chateau a few miles from Paris, in which was a room of state, fitted up in the most splendid manner imaginable.

It was evening when I was conducted to this place, where I found the Duchess dressed in the habit of a girl from head to foot. She told me I was like the Dauphiness,* then just arrived, and whom she loved to distraction; that she would, now she was acquainted with my passion for exercising the rod, be highly delighted with the pleasure from my hands. Here, my dear, said she, are some written instructions, which I beg you will look over with attention, and then I will conduct you to the dressing-room.

---

* We hope the authoress will excuse us, but we cannot mention real titles or names throughout this work.
* Now Queen of F———.

These instructions will appear through my story.

As soon as I had folded the paper, she led me to her dressing-room, where she had the richest dresses I ever beheld. Out of these she selected what was agreeable to her passion, and helped to dress me, and in about an hour I found myself bending under a weight of silk, jewels, and every other ornament that could add a charm to beauty. As soon as I was dressed she led me to a room, where her sister, six other ladies, and a lady who had the appearance of a full-grown girl, were sitting, who, on my entrance, arose, and paid their respects in the same manner as though I had been a Queen. The truth is they fancied me such.

Being complete mistress of my instructions, I challenged the girl about telling lies, who denied the accusation, and was proved criminal by the ladies, one of whom instantly put a rod into my hand and begged I would make a proper use of it. She was instantly horsed by the Cometess of ——, a very stout woman, and I whipped her to her own satisfaction, and to that of those around me.

As soon as I had done, I enquired for her sister, who I understood, by my instructions, was a greater culprit, and who had left the room as soon as I had done (this was no other than the Duchess). I was told she was not to be found. I dispatched three of my attendants after her, and with the remainder I repaired to the room of state.

This was the most splendid room I ever beheld. The canopy and chairs of state were of the most magnificent kind, and in the chandeliers and girandoles there could not be less than five hundred lights.

According to my instructions I took my seat on the throne, with my maids of honour on each side, and in a few minutes my bold step-daughter was brought in in tears.

Her entreaties were of the most extravagant kind, such as kissing my hands and feet, and embracing me, all which I was inattentive to, and instantly ordered my maids of honour to hand me the rod.

A frame was rolled before the throne, made sloping like a desk, on which was a large white satin cushion, and on which, with the assistance of a little stool, she was extended and held down.

It was now, according to my directions, my business to unveil the seat of pleasure, which, with some struggles on her part, I instantly did, and I think I never beheld posteriors more beautiful! They were the largest, plumpest, and whitest, that ever felt a rod from my hand.

The burthen of her supplication, looking back at me the whole time, was, "My dear Mamma, my lovely Queen Mamma, pray pardon me! Indeed, you'll find me a most excellent girl in future, and I protest to you, upon my honour, I never will provoke you to take the rod in your beautiful, angelic hand again! I'll bless the hour you married my Papa, my lovely sweet Queen, and love you the longest day I live, if you will forgive me this time!" Such was the language she made use of in reply to my lecture, which continued for full ten minutes, in concert with the rod, which (as instructed) I made excellent use of, I assure you. As soon as I found she had enough, she was let down by my directions, and she retired crying.

I continued in the apartment, chatting with two of the ladies (for the remainder went out with her) for about an hour, when she entered in full dress, and looked divinely.

As soon as she entered, she cried out in a great passion for the rod, which, she recollected, was taken to another room.

While she was in pursuit of it, one of the ladies told me she meant to personate the Empress of R., and that I must drop my own character, and take up that of her daughter.

I complied with the desire, and in less than a minute she entered with great dignity, having her train supported by two ladies.

She charged me with abusive expressions I had dropped concerning her beauty; and without giving me time to reply, she took me by the arm, and led me to the seat of chastisement, where, with the assistance of her maids, I was extended.

After she had raised my clothes above the small of my back, it was full a minute before I felt the rod. She put herself in the greatest passion imaginable, stamped, and called to one of the ladies for the instrument with which she was to wreak her vengeance. I had taken notice while I whipped her, that she bawled and roared with very little intermission during the whole time, which led me to suppose it eased in some measure the smart, which she convinced me of in a few minutes, for she whipped with great severity, throwing herself into the most wanton attitudes I every beheld. Indeed, I was obliged to bawl in good earnest, for I had never received anything like the punishment before. She took care not to put this into the instructions she gave me, else I would not have undergone it. I must own I like it as well as any lady present, but not with such severity; that I leave to the men, many of whom I have read lye under the lash till they bleed.

Your story, said Miss V., has much whimsicality in it, indeed, more than ever I heard. The only anecdote that ever I heard that approaches it is that of Miss G.

Miss G. was a woman passionately fond of whipping boys and girls. She was the daughter of an officer, and received a very polished education: add to this she was in possession of every requisite to make an excellent school-mistress. She was tall, well made, very fair, expressive blue eyes; she had also that haughty and severe look that men delight in who are fond of tasting the rod from the hand of a woman. Her father and mother dying when she was about twenty, and leaving her without fortune, she came to London, and went as an assistant in a distinguished young ladies' boarding-school. Here she gave a loose to her passion, for there was scarce a day she did not whip half-a-dozen young girls,* some of them fourteen years old.

Lord —— going one day to see a cousin of his who was a boarder at that school, saw this lady by chance, and was so captivated with her beauty that he offered her a carte blanche, which she closed with, and the connexion lasted during his life.

Passing one day through St. James's Park, she met Miss C., an eminent milliner (from whom I had the tale). As they had been very intimate school-fellows, Miss G. after a few turns asked her to dine with her, which she accepted.

Lord —— being then at Paris, they dined alone. While they were talking about the fashion, Miss C. perceiving in the corner of the room a large birch-rod hanging from a nail, asked for whom it was intended; she smiling told her if she would come the day after to drink tea with her, she would tell her the use of it.

Miss C. did not fail to come. She found Miss G. dressed in a very splendid manner, as she intended to go

---

* We believe the authoress is in error here, for it has been affirmed by many who have seen her manuscript, that there is no birch discipline used in any boarding-school. Of this the ladies are best judges.

to the Pantheon that evening. Her hair was dressed in the extreme of the fashion, excessively large and low behind, and ornamented with a panache of black and white feathers of the largest size. — Very high on the left side of her bosom she wore an enormous bouquet of natural flowers, which had a beautiful effect. After dinner she rung the bell for her maid, and desired the two young ladies might be sent down from the nursery. In a few minutes, two fine girls, one about thirteen and the other eleven, made their appearance.

Well, ladies, said Miss G., who passed for their step-mother, shew me your work. — On finding it badly done, she boxed their ears very well. — Let me see now if you can say the lesson I gave you this morning in the grammar. Finding the youngest very deficient in it, she flew into a violent passion, bounced away directly for the rod, and protested with great passion she would whip her severely.

Miss C. pretended to save the young culprit, but in vain; — the disciplinarian made some apologies for whipping her before her, but the minx was so very indolent and bold, she must absolutely whip her well.

Turn up your petticoats this moment, you little idle

hussey (said she, brandishing the rod); I'll teach you this time to mind what I say! Come, come, higher still, and lye down across my knee.

Oh, mother, mother, my dear lovely mother! said the little creature (as the lady was exposing her posteriors to the rod), upon my honour I'll be a most excellent girl in future; try me but this once, and if every I give you this trouble again I will give you leave to cut me to pieces.

No, said the enraged lady, I am resolved to whip you smartly this time. I have taken uncommon pains in your education, and you are now as bad as a girl of three years old. I have your pretty bottom this time to my wish, and you shall now feel it smart.

Didn't you promise me you'd be more diligent? Indeed, Mamma, I did, and you will find me so, believe me. — Yes, yes, yes, yes, so I suppose, for a few days after this whipping. Oh, Mamma! Oh, my dear, dear Mamma! Oh, for God's sake let me down! — I will not, upon my honour, till I have exercised this rod to my liking! You shall caper a little longer, my pretty Miss, I assure you! Your last mother was either too proud or too lazy to take the rod in hand, and left you to the correction of her maid; but you soon found a mother in me, whose greatest pleasure is having bold boys and girls in this situation, and whip, whip, whip, whipping them well.

Instead of minding your book, you are romping with your impudent sister, who I thought got a whipping yesterday she would remember some time, but she shall get one more to my liking soon as I am done with you, she may rest assured of!

I dare say you never felt the rod so charming from any other hand?

No, indeed, my dear, dear Mamma, pray let me down. Will you mind your work in future? Yes, indeed, indeed I will.

You are certain of it? I am indeed, my sweet, lovely Mamma.

There, go to the nursery, and don't let me see your face till you can convince me you have mended your manners.

Her manner of treating the other young lady was similar, and she was sent in tears to keep her sister company.

Well, said Miss G., when the culprits had retired, don't you think I would make an excellent governess? Most certainly, said Miss C., who had been quite delighted with her exquisite manner of handling the rod. I own, said Miss G., I take a very particular pleasure in whipping children when bold; and since the age of fifteen, that an aunt of mine made me whip a little girl about nine years of age, who lived with us, this passion has been predominant in me. This little girl was the daughter of my nurse, and one of the most stubborn little girls I ever met with. The old lady made me whip her, she said, to teach me how to whip children when I should have some of my own.

I took so much pleasure in whipping that little girl, that there were few days I did not take the rod in hand, having many opportunities, as I taught her to read and write.

I grew so fond of it, I really would be unhappy now if I had not some children under my care on whom I could inflict this punishment: though I declare to you I would not take the least pleasure in it in cold blood; I must be provoked to it, and they must deserve it fairly.

Miss C. had several young apprentices, on some of which she inflicted the punishment of the rod. She was not sorry when they gave her an opportunity of handling this instrument of pleasure and pain. Among her apprentices was a slip of a girl, addicted to thieving, and though she had whipped her very often for it with severity, the girl did not amend in the least. One day as she was going to whip her for stealing some ribbons, one of the working women, who had been in Paris for many years, told her, if she was to dip the rod in vinegar, as she had seen it done in France, it would smart her the more. Miss C. followed her advice, dipped the end of a new birch-rod in a vessel full of vinegar, and whipped the girl with it with the utmost exertion of her arm; and it smarted so sore that she never pilfered after.

Miss C. visited Miss G. pretty often. Having observed that Miss G. wore constantly an enormous nosegay, she asked the reason of it, as if the flowers did not give her the head-ache? Not at all, said she, I am passionately fond of them — their sweet perfume excites in me the most exquisite sensations. She told her Lord —— was as fond of them as she, and delighted in seeing her dressed with a very large one. She knew many gentlemen who were equally as fond of them as his lordship, and delighted in seeing their favourite ladies dressed with them; that the larger and fuller they are, the greater their influence, especially when worn very high on the left side, the luxurious mode of wearing them. Wearing them in centre, as some ladies do, is very inelegant; but on one side, as the French do, gives not only a grand but a voluptuous air to the wearer; and it is looked on now in the fashionable world as one of the greatest incentives to the joys of Venus. Some people even look upon them as great a provocative as birch itself; and that, not only physicians on the continent, but many in this country, prescribe for sterile* men and women. Indeed, a certain

---

* The following anecdote, to illustrate this passage, is a fact:— A country gentleman, of large fortune, had been married for many years to a very beautiful, and seemingly fruitful, woman. The want of children was the only thing that made them unhappy. When the lady arrived in London, a few winters ago, she patronized a very sensible and beautiful opera-dancer, to whom, in a private conversation, she expressed her uneasiness about her sterility, or her husband's incapacity. The Italian lady told her nothing was so efficacious as whipping the posteriors of her husband (if the fault lay in him) during the amorous engagement with her; and to prove her assertion true, she repeated the physician's anecdote from the Philosophical Theresa, and strengthened it with assuring her she herself assisted in a similar scene. The lady pondered on it, related it to her husband, and prevailed on him to go through the operation. The lady was engaged at a high price to administer the rod, which she did in that opera-dress that pleased him most; and, in less than a month, and by the time she whipped him a dozen times (each space of which he was in an amorous engagement with his wife), the lady, to her great joy, found herself pregnant.

doctor assured the world, that in order to get beautiful children, men should enjoy women in their full dress, or any dress they liked best, or as they were when they fell in love with them; not forgetting to have them highly perfumed, and with large bouquets of the most odoriferous flowers in their bosom — their secret influence being astonishing. The ladies on the continent are seldom seen without very large nosegays, which they always wear on the left side, as high as the ear.

A young lady of my acquaintance, who was lately in Lisbon, being invited to a dance given by a lady on her name's-day, which answers to our birth-day, all the ladies came dressed with enormous nosegays; not only their left bosom, but their faces were covered with them. However, when they were dancing it had a pretty effect. Those large nosegays, I have been told, are very useful in hot countries, where perspiration is very great.

Your observations on the flowers are very just, said Lady C. I am well acquainted with many of the same disposition.

Mr. D., a gentleman of fortune, excessively fond of seeing the rod exercised, and feeling it too, advertised for a governess to instruct his three daughters, their French governess having returned to Paris.

Miss F., a young Irish lady, very pretty, and very much reduced (having made a *faux-pas* with a young officer), applied for the place.

Mr. D., finding her a great advocate for the rod, engaged her immediately. She was the daughter of Mrs. F., a schoolmistress in Dublin. Educated under such a mother, Miss F. was complete mistress of birch-discipline, and as passionately fond of it as any woman in England.

A few days after she had been at Mr. D.'s seat, as she was going early in the morning to take a walk in the garden, Mr. D. perceived and followed her. She was in a half-mourning dress, with a large French nightcap, her hair very large and low behind. Their conversation chiefly turned on the sweet perfume of the flowers; the gentleman proposed to make a nosegay for her sweet angelic bosom, and in a few minutes presented her with one as big as a broom. Miss F. was quite delighted with it, and instantly tied it very high on the left side of her bosom, for she was very well acquainted with their influence.

Mr. D. paid her many compliments — said she looked

divine, and called her his angelic governess!

She thought it was now high time to introduce the favourite subject. She informed him that one of his nieces had been very bold, and that she intended to whip her. Mr. D. squeezed her delicate hand, and apologized for the trouble she would be at. Don't talk of that, my dear Sir; I like to whip bold girls — and bold boys too (giving him a very significant look), especially when I can get a good birch-rod. Mr. D. conducted her to the shrubbery, where there were several birch trees. She immediately made two excellent rods, and of a large size; for she was very fond (as many ladies are) to whip with large rods, as they make a greater sound on the b—, a sound very pleasing to the votaries of whipping, and gives a woman a severe air; besides large rods don't hurt so much as small ones that cut shockingly. As soon as she came to the house, she went to the working-room, and calling the young culprit to her, a girl about thirteen, Here is, Miss, shaking her big rod, something that will make you good! Come, come! up with your frock and petticoats! I must see all; come, kiss the rod, and beg a good whipping. Then holding her upon her lap, she whipped her for full ten minutes. Mr. D., who was in an adjacent room peeping through a hole, was all the time in a kind of ecstasy! He had never seen a woman whip with so much grace! Her dress, especially her monstrous bouquet, which she was smelling all the while, made her look most charmingly! As soon as she had done, he flew to her, and spent with her a most delicious hour. This lady used to assume with him the character of a severe aunt. While she whipped him, he held himself in such a manner, that he could smell the bouquet all the time. I have been told that a great many men do the same, their pleasure being much heightened by it.

Miss L., another votary to birch-discipline, was the daughter of a clergyman, who kept a school at ——. Her mother dying when she was about thirteen, her father, as she was very clever, and very tall for her age, gave her the care of her sisters; as they were very giddy, she got leave from her father to whip them. She grew so fond of the birch, that she found means to get other young girls to instruct, and on whom she administered, very often, the rod. Her father dying when she was about two-and-twenty, she came to town, opened a young ladies' boarding-school, and in a few years got a very large school. She then gave a loose to her favourite passion, whipping sometimes a dozen girls a-day. As she was an experienced hand at whipping, she seldom dismissed them till their posteriors and thighs were as red as scarlet. Her pleasure was to cut them, and generally whipped till the blood would come. She continued that practice till they were at least fifteen. Many mothers approved of her conduct very much. She had a closet full of birch-rods of different sizes, curiously bound with ribbons of different colours.

She took a singular pleasure in choosing the long slender twigs of the birch with buds on them, and binding them up in rods; she never used the rod twice, nor any birch but what was cut lately. The smell of new birch raised in her the most pleasing sensation. After she had whipped a girl, she always made her wear the rod in her bosom as a nosegay for two or three hours.

The Hon. Mr. S., at the age of seventeen, had a beautiful sister a year younger than him. She married Lord ——. Their father and mother being dead, they lived with an old aunt. Mr. S. was then at Oxford, but came to town very often. He had taken notice of his sister whipping very often a pretty cousin, a girl about ten years old, who was under her care. One day as he was reading in his sister's room a French book about women being fond of whipping, which he had found on her toilet, he heard her coming with her cousin, who was then crying; suspecting she was going to whip her, he hid himself behind the curtain of the bed: he was not mistaken; his sister immediately entering with a good birch-rod in her hand. Petticoats, &c., were all soon removed. After whipping her severely, and lecturing her all the time, as an experienced school-mistress, she sent her down stairs, and soon went herself as if nothing had happened.

Mr. D. declared to a friend of his that he never saw anything so pretty, his sister being dressed that day all in white, with a large pink sash round her waist; her hair, which was not yet turned up, wantonly flowing on her snowy bosom, which was heaving all the time; a pretty hat on one side of the head, full of large white ostrich feathers, and a beautiful bouquet of a most enormous size, made of moss-roses, carnations, pinks intermixed with large bunches of myrtle, jessamy, and minionet, which she wore on the left-side, up to the ear. The exquisite perfume of it excited in him such agreeable sensations that after that he would never bear his sister or any young lady of his acquaintance without a monstrous one. The waving of the feathers, the shaking of the flowers of the nosegay, the sound of the birch, and especially the exquisite perfume which the bouquet exhaled, had such an effect on him that he remained for an hour in a sort of ecstasy. He had a garden entirely laid out with the most beautiful sweet flowers imaginable. He used to send out of it to his female acquaintance large bouquets that he might have the pleasure to see them dress well at the public places where he knew he would meet with them; to tie himself a nosegay for the bosom of a lady was a delight to him. His seeing one day a lady at the Pantheon, the beautiful Miss W., with a most enormous side-bouquet, whose pretty face could scarce be seen among the flowers, he fell in love with her, and married her about a month after; she was but fourteen then, and just out of school.

On the continent, where whipping is so fashionable, it is one of the chief amusements of the Nuns, for they not only whip one another for their pleasure, but will whip with shocking birch-rods their boarders, with so much severity, that sometimes some of them are obliged to keep their beds for two or three days; this is a fact, and many young ladies who have been educated there would assert it. I was always surprised not to meet with any book which would lay open the incontinency of the Nuns; for some Nuns take as much pleasure in whipping a pretty girl, with the help of a certain curious instrument, as they would almost to sleep with a man, and have almost the same pleasure.

Your anecdote, said Mrs. ——, brings to my recollection a particular whim of Lady Dowager ——.

This woman, who had been considered one of the first beauties of her time, fell desperately in love with a lady's-maid, where she had been on a visit, at a time when the fire of youth might be supposed to be in a great measure extinguished, for she had passed her fiftieth year. She had tasted the felicity we have been speaking of from numbers of her confidential friends, and took as great a pleasure in administering it as any lady existing.

This Abigail enflamed her the instant she beheld her, and she lost no time to secure her to herself, which she did at a great salary.

I have heard her ladyship declare no school-mistress upon earth could exercise the rod with more bewitching severity than this woman. It was her ladyship's whim to be whipp'd by her in the neat habiliments of an upper servant.

Sometimes she would desire her to enter her apartment with a neat straw hat, set off with a vast quantity of pink or green ribbon, a pretty flowered gown, and her legs and feet as neatly attired. She used to act at such a time as her mother's-maid, and whip her ladyship for telling tales of her while she had been abroad.

Her ladyship being a very fat woman, it was next to an impossibility for her to lye across her lap (though that is what she delighted in), but she commonly rested her hands on a sopha or chair, but oftener would have herself whipped in bed for not getting up early, which I take of all others to be the pleasantest way, as we can then bounce and plunge about, struggle and caper under the rod, and prolong the felicity for a considerable time.

No youth, though ever so enraptured with his charmer, could idolize her more than her ladyship did this woman. I have heard her dwell upon the beauty of her hands, and the heaving of her plump snowy bosom, till she had been lost in excess of bliss. She died in her ladyship's service, and she often declared a great part of her happiness died with her.

A Duchess in Paris, who has tasted of this felicity from the hands of a vast number of ladies of her own complexion, took an uncommon liking to a beautiful West-India negro woman, who had been brought to Paris by a naval officer, from whom she was purchased at an high price by her for this purpose. As soon as she was in possession of her she spared no expense in educating her, and clothed her in the most elegant manner. When she fancied she was polished at all points for her purpose she broke the matter to her, and, with the assistance of a number of books and prints on the subject, instructed her perfectly. She often declared to a female confidante, nothing could equal the pleasure she felt when this lovely negro stripped her or took her out of bed; to feel her velvet hands run over her thighs and posteriors when she settling her on her knees, and immediately after the rod smartly exercised by her, was to her the height of human pleasure. This woman, strange as it may appear, had such an ascendancy over this illustrious lady, that she was in a short while mistress of her affection and fortune. — I have been well assured a gentleman now in London has a pretty negro maid-servant, and his greatest delight is to see her whip his children.

The spirit of flagellation, said Mrs. W., was never carried to such an high degree as it is in a particular school this day in London. — I never heard of this school before, said Miss T., pray where is it? It is kept by Mademoiselle G—— who lives in —— street, B—y— Square. This lady about twelve years ago made her appearance in this kingdom, and was recommended to the Countess of ——, who instantly patronized her.

At one of their nocturnal meetings, when her ladyship's whipping party were all present, and were all running out in raptures on the graces and lovely manœuvres of Ma'emoiselle while whipping each, the Countess proposed a singular affair which every lady instantly subscribed to. It was no other than Ma'emoiselle's setting up a day-school to teach genteel children French. They opened a subscription instantly for the Parisian lady, enabled her to take a house, and furnished it for her in an elegant style. Not one of the party were seen in this business; their only patronage was a heavy purse, for a very substantial reason that will

appear in its proper place. The lady had not opened
school three months when she found herself at the head
of a pretty set of children, many of whom were full
grown. A short while after she opened this seminary one
of the whipping party appeared as a sub-governess, in
which capacity she indulged herself to her with,
exercising the rod as she thought proper. The other
ladies were engaged by Ma'emoiselle to fill the same
character alternately.*

What a treat in this seminary for the idolators of the
posterior shrine! To see in the course of a day a number
of b—s blushing under the rod, exercised by a woman of
supereminent charms!

It must be the sublime of felicity indeed, said Miss T.,
and almost equal to what I tasted from the hand of Lady
—— a few days ago.

I know, said Mrs. W., her ladyship is charming in the
extreme with a rod in her hand. Pray let us hear how she

---

* One of the party, lately deceased, observing extraordinary
signs of manhood in a boy, as he lay across her lap capering
under the rod, was so smitten with the prospect, that she had
it in view as often as she could, and ere the youth had gained
his fifteenth year she made him ample amends for the
whipping he received from her hands, by an offering of the
most sublime nature in the chapel of Venus.

captivated you?

I happened to pay her a visit in my military habit, which so pleased her that she proposed to take the rod in hand and whip me for endeavouring to rival her, my step-mother, by dressing in such alluring habiliments.

Her sister, Louisa, happened to be present, who seconded the motion, and I instantly ran up stairs to the room where I knew she kept her horse. They both followed. — Louisa, at the head of the machine, held my hands, while her ladyship, with her usual manœuvres, exposed what she idolized so much to the rod, and indeed I felt the full force of her jealousy (by my endeavouring to outdo her in dress) while she exercised the bewitching twigs. In brief, my dear ladies, I think no woman in the whole circle of beauty has it in her power to captivate like this lovely creature; everything that has been said by the poets in praise of female charms, falls far short of what I see in her! Her admirers may well exclaim—

> What thought can paint that fair perfection?
> Not sea-born Venus, in the courts beneath,
> When the green nymphs first kissed her coral lips,
> All polished fair, and wash'd with orient beauty,

Could in their dazling fancy match her brightness,

Her legs, her arms, her hands, her neck, her breasts,

So nicely shap'd, so matchless in their lustre,

Such all perfection!——

She is the child of love, and she was born in smiles!

To hear the music of her voice while correcting me was something more than human. I shall never forget her "Well, upon my honour, it is to me surprising how some mothers will suffer their forward daughters to eclipse them, while there is such a rod as I hold to be found. I have heard, Miss, you put on this dress to captivate Colonel G——; but I'll teach you to consult me in future about what you shall wear! Your pretty b—e shall feel my resentment before I have done with the rod, I promise you! You may caper as much as you please, but you'll find me exercise it well! Yes, yes, yes, yes, yes! you forward minx!"

Stop, my dear, for heaven's sake, said Mrs. W., else you will so transport us that we shall rush like lunatics to her ladyship for a sample of what you tasted.

I called to see our lovely brunette, Mrs. C., a few mornings ago, and found her busily employed with the rod. Her nephew and niece were found wrangling together by her, and she settled their difference with giving each an excellent whipping. — I have heard this charming Creole protest she would be very unhappy if she had not some children to divert herself with in this way. She has declared to me when she was in Jamaica, she used to amuse herself almost every day with whipping pretty young negroes of both sexes. She has ever given the preference to whipping boys under eight years old. — I remember an anecdote of this lady that made me laugh heartily at the time. One day, while she was at her brother's country house, a beggar woman came into the yard with two children, who solicited her charity. She ordered them into the house, and relieved them. They had scarcely left the house when a spoon was missed, which was found on a girl of twelve years old. She was brought back; and by her order was brought on the shoulders of a stout maid-servant into the parlour. Her brother was present, who applauded her highly for her spirit. In less than a minute she removed the poor girl's rags, and exposed to his view as fair and as plump a bumfiddle as Venus herself could exhibit, which in a few minutes the lady left in weals, with a rod exercised with the utmost severity. But think how great this lady's surprise must be to have pointed out to her in Covent Garden Theatre, within these three months, this very girl, who has been in keeping with her brother from the day of her being whipped to this.

As to mankind being fond of this pleasure from the hands of a woman, it is too well confirmed to be contradicted. I have read the fashionable Lectures, and a number of French anecdotes relating to this passion, and I think I can communicate from my own knowledge a more striking one than any I have ever read or heard.

Come, disclose, disclose, my dear, said half-a-dozen ladies at once.

To be brief, ladies, said Miss T., that libidinous gentleman, Mr. K., who is known to many in this room, is so passionately fond of birch from a lady, that his *Wards*, who live with him, exercise it whenever they want money, elegant clothes, or see pleasure. He has a room remote from the noise and interruption of his domestics. — Here, whenever he refused what they request, he is led by these spirited and whimsical girls; and here they strip and whip him, turn about, till he promises to comply with their request. When the eldest of these pretty girls disclosed the affair to me, I would not give it credit, nor would I to this hour, if I had not ocular demonstration, about three months ago, when they concealed me in a closet, in the room, from a peep-hole in which I beheld the whole discipline.

Here ends the anecdotes of this lady, which many will think written with spirit and elegance: this, with their originality, will secure them a distinguished reception among those who idolize, with a degree of religious enthusiasm, the beautiful back settlements of Venus.

F I N I S.

Part Two

PART THE SECOND

OF THE

EXHIBITION

OF

FEMALE FLAGELLANTS

IN THE

Modest and Incontinent World.

Proving from Indubitable F A C T S,
That a Number of LADIES take a SECRET PLEASURE,
In W H I P P I N G their own,
AND CHILDREN COMMITTED TO THEIR CARE;
AND THAT THEIR P A S S I O N
FOR EXERCISING AND FEELING THE EXQUISITE
P L E A S U R E OF A BIRCH-ROD,
FROM OBJECTS OF THEIR CHOICE.
OF BOTH SEXES,
IS TO THE FULL AS PREDOMINANT,
AS THAT OF MANKIND.

Now First Publifhed from a LADY'S Manufcript, and a Number of Letters fent to the EDITOR of the Firft Part of this original Work.

LONDON:
Printed for G. Peacock, No. 66 Drury Lane.

MDCCLXXXV.

PRELIMINARY ADDRESS.

WHEN the First Part of this singular and original Work was published, there was very little expected from the sale after the Subscribers had their copies. The singularity of the Work was talked of, particularly among the Ladies, and it was owing to their curiosity, no doubt, the sale became extensive. Much has been said pro *and* con *about the authenticity of the anecdotes; and some readers have been found silly enough to declare, because the passion is not natural, and does not run in the common channel, there can be no truth in it. Now a man who absolutely loves a fine woman, will not love her the less for exhibiting her bumfiddle to his enraptured sight! Nay, should she request a sample from his hands, of what her mother or governess often gave her when guilty of a crime, where is the mighty error? 'Tis but a whipping, and if she chooses it from the fair hand of a woman, or from the opposite sex, I cannot see how the moral world can be injured by it. Her bumfiddle is as much her own as any other fiddle, and it would be hard indeed if she was prevented from having her favourite musician to play upon it whenever she thought proper.*

ANECDOTES and LECTURES

FOR THE

SECOND PART

OF THE

Female Flagellants

WITH

T A L E S,

Translated from the FRENCH.

To the AUTHORESS of the Female Flagellants.

MADAM,

I HAVE read with pleasure your exhibition, &c.; but (between us) I think you should have dwelt a little more on the lectures, as in your fashionable ones. I was very much pleased, as well as several ladies of my acquaintance, with the description of the dress of the characters, particularly with those that wore large nosegays. A pretty woman with a very large bouquet on one side of her bosom, is to many men a most heavenly object. I send you a few real anecdotes, which, if you will take the trouble of embellishing, might be added to a second part of the exhibition, &c., or of the fashionable lectures.

Yours,

C. D.

Miss N., a young lady of my acquaintance, was, at a very early age, so fond of birch discipline, that she would sometimes take her Mamma's rod, and exercise it with pleasure on her doll: she could never account for that whimsical passion. Her mother dying when she was about eighteen, she went to live with an aunt, who had under her care two girls about twelve years old — distant relations of hers. As they were very wild and indolent, Miss N. advised her to whip them with a birch-rod; but she, being rather infirm, requested she would ease her of the trouble, and take the care of them on herself. This was what Miss N. wanted; she soon gave a loose to her favourite passion; and no felicity on earth, she thought, could equal the pleasure she felt when whipping the bums of her young pupils. One day she went to visit a friend of hers, that lived about five miles from town, and had been married lately to a gentleman of fortune, a widower with one daughter. She found her busy making a rod, and asked her if she had any bold children in the house? Yes, my dear, I was just going to whip my step-daughter for telling a lye — it is a thing I never forgive: and, if you will excuse me, I will go and give it to her, for I hate, of all things, to defer correcting children when they deserve it; and without waiting for an answer, she opened the door of a back parlour, where a beautiful girl, about thirteen, was sobbing and crying. After turning up her petticoats as high as the small of her back, she whipped her with a great deal of severity. Miss N. took notice how she squeezed her between her thighs all the time, as she whipped her standing, leaning only against a bureau. After she had done she took Miss N. to the garden, and picked for her a beautiful nosegay, but so monstrously large that she was almost ashamed to wear it. However, as her friend wore one of an equal size, she pinned it to her bosom. I see, my dear, said she, you are not acquainted with the secret influence of flowers; know, my dear girl, that their sweet perfume has an uncommon effect on many men and women; but to have that effect on men, they must adorn a lovely bosom like yours. After spending a very agreeable evening, Miss N., being told the coach was at the door, took her leave. She was not gone a mile, when a servant in livery stopped the coachman, to know if his master, Sir G. B., a gentleman as great a votary to Flora as to birch discipline, could have a place in the coach — one of the wheels of his own having broke on the road. Miss N. was too civil to refuse; and the gentleman soon made his appearance, and apologized for his intrusion. He was struck with her beauty, for she was really a most elegant woman, and paid her many compliments; said she looked most charmingly, praised very much her nosegay, and, in his opinion, nothing could be more becoming. At their parting, he requested permission to visit her, which she granted. A few days after, a servant came with a large blooming nosegay, as big as a broom, and a note to know if she would be at home in the evening, and to request her acceptance of the bouquet. She answered that she and her aunt would be glad of his company at tea. Whilst she was dressing, one of the girls came to complain that her sister had scratched and beaten her terribly. As soon as she was dressed, she came down with Sir G——'s bouquet in her bosom; and, after making out of a new broom a most excellent rod, she took the bold hussey to her room, pinned her smock to her shoulders, and holding her fast between her thighs, her leg over hers, she began to whip her as hard as she could, leaning her back against the edge of a table, as she had seen her friend do. I have been told that the fair votaries of birch discipline prefer that attitude to any other. — Will you beat your sister again, said she; will you, will you, will you, will you, will you, will you, you little spiteful slut? — Indeed, indeed, cousin, I never will do it again; pray do forgive me. — I won't forgive you till I humble your proud spirit, you little vixen; I'll whip, whip, whip, whip, whip, whip, whip this bold a—e to my liking. What made you scratch your sister? — tell, tell, tell, tell, tell, tell, tell me this minute. — It was she that began first; oh dear, you hurt me shockingly! — I am glad to hear it — yes, yes, yes, yes, yes, yes, yes, yes! I will make a good girl of you, and make you feel this excellent rod! What a fine spring it has! new birch, I see, is the only thing for whipping bold girls with; and this imprudent bum shall get, get, get, get, get, get, get, get enough of it, I promise you! I am resolved to whip your a—e so well, that you shall remember it a long time. Will you be more diligent, and not be always romping instead of minding your work — will you, will you, will you, will you, will you, will you, will you, you little minx? will you ever scratch your sister again — tell me, tell, tell, tell, tell, tell, tell me? — Oh, no! indeed I never will — forgive me this once; oh, pray do! — Will you be very good for the future? Indeed I will. — Are you sure of it? — are you, are you, are you? If ever you beat your sister again, I will whip you till the blood comes. Go along, you bold slut!

Miss N. declared to a friend, that between the fragrance of the flowers, and the pleasure of exercising the rod, she felt inexpressible delight! No wonder, for the tears of concupiscence, as she confessed, fell in abundance on the spot where she whipped her, and said she never had so much pleasure in whipping before, which she attributed to the sweet odour of her bouquet. She had scarce done, when Sir G. was announced, and was quite enraptured to see in her bosom the bouquet he sent her, especially as she wore it so high on the left side of her bosom, that her pretty face was half shaded with it. After tea, Miss A., a smart young lady about seventeen, an acquaintance of Miss N., called to see her — she was uncommonly well dressed, and happened to have also in her bosom a very large nosegay of moss roses, carnations, jessamy, &c. Sir G. was quite delighted, and gazed on them both with rapture. After some trifling conversation, they all agreed to go to the Opera. When it was over, he took the young ladies home in his coach — left Miss A. at her own house; and, as soon as he was alone with Miss N., declared his passion. She promised to give him an answer in three days. At the appointed time he waited on her, and was shewn into a parlour, where, while he was waiting for his charmer, he perceived behind the glass a birch-rod. As one of the young girls happened to be in the parlour at work, he soon got from her all the information he desired concerning it, which delighted him very much, and determined him to make Miss N. his wife as soon as possible. She soon made her appearance in an elegant deshabille; he earnestly entreated her to name the happy day, which she did after some hesitation; and I had the pleasure of hearing that their nuptials soon took place. She took the young girls home with her, as Sir G. said he would provide for them. One day, as she was going to a ball, elegantly dressed in a white lutestring, beautifully trimmed with crape and flowers; on the side of her head a black gauze hat, looped up with a brilliant loop and button, and ornamented with nine large white ostrich feathers; her hair dressed very high and wide to the front, the chignon very large and low, and highly perfumed; her snowy bosom quite bare, except what was covered by an immense side bouquet, exhaling a most exquisite perfume; her lovely hands adorned with elegant bracelets, &c., one of the girls committed in her presence a very heavy offence; and, wishing to correct her before she went, she called her husband to help her, as the girl was very ungovernable, and she was unwilling to tumble her dress. He, quite delighted, immediately complied with her request, made her sit on his lap, taking care *de tui mettre en levrette*, while she was employed in turning up the petticoats of the young culprit, who was too much frightened to see anything; then holding the girl's hands with one of his, while the other pressed the waist of his dear flagellator, who, almost lost in bliss, was whipping the little minx with the utmost severity. She was so well pleased that day, that she generally found the assistance of her husband necessary when any of them deserved chastisement. I have been told that there are some young ladies fond of administering the birch discipline, that will contrive to put in a certain place a curious instrument, which very much heightens their felicity, especially when the child kicks and plunges.

After taking a pleasant ride one evening last summer, I alighted at the house of a particular female friend who had been about six months married. Her husband had three children by a former wife, two of which I found her reprimanding with great heat when I entered, and who kept up a continued roar the whole time, though she had not taken the rod in hand, nor did she then intend it, as she did not choose to spoil her dress, which was beautiful in the highest degree. She intended to appear at the Opera that evening, and she took uncommon pains to captivate the fashionable youth, by wearing a fancy dress enough to raise an inextinguishable flame in the breast of an Anchoret.

When I found she had no notion of taking the rod in hand, I enforced the utility of it very strongly, which she agreed to, with a request that I might give her blubbering son a good whipping, while she tickled sulky Miss's posteriors. She brought from her closet a rod rather of the largest size, which we divided between us, and she having got roaring Miss under her arm, with her posteriors well bared to the rod, and I Master's trowsers down, which I had some difficulty in doing, he struggled and plunged so much on my lap, we did not cease whipping till we left their bums as nicely marked with the rod as any enraged schoolmistress could do it. What with the harmony of this angelic woman's voice while lecturing her daughter — her dress from head to foot — the brilliancy of her eyes, which shot their fire into my very soul and set it in a blaze — her fair skin and plump swelling bosom, with two heavenly dimples in her cheeks — all these powerful provocatives, with that of exercising the rod on the boy, almost deprived me of my senses, and scarce knowing what I did, as soon as the children went down stairs, I threw myself at the feet of the adorable flagellator and kissed them with rapture; then, starting up, embraced her, and begged the felicity from her magic hand.

Pleasure sparkled in her eyes as soon as I had made the request, and having placed me across two chairs, and exposed my swelling bum, she exercised the rod with the most bewitching severity imaginable, using with a little variation much the same lecture she delivered to her daughter, which was pretty nearly in the following words:—

Will you for ever provoke me to take the rod in hand, you bold vixen! I thought the whipping I gave you yesterday morning would make you remember what I can do with a rod! — Indeed, my dear lovely Mamma, it was my brother's fault, he does nothing but quarrel with me from morning till night! I don't believe but you are as quarrelsome as he, and I am determined to whip, whip, whip, whip this stubborn spirit out of you! yes, yes, yes, yes, you naughty girl! O my sweet Mamma, pray forgive me, pray do! No, no, no, no, I will not, upon my honour! Your Papa told me a few days after I married him, he did not believe your own Mamma ever gave you a taste of a rod, but I was resolved the first opportunity, which happened the next day, to make you dance to some tune, under as good a rod as this I exercise now! Yes, yes, yes, yes, you bold, impudent girl! And you shall find I'll take it in hand with as good a will while I have strength to conquer your turbulent spirit! O dear! O Mamma! O dear, dear Mamma! my lovely, sweet, charming Mamma, pray, pray, pray forgive me! don't whip me any more! I'll kiss the rod indeed, and promise you, upon my honour, never to give you this trouble again! Are, are, are, are you sure of it? Do, my lovely, dear, sweet Mamma, try me this once, and you'll find me a most excellent girl, you will, upon my honour! — Well, I'll try you: here, kiss the rod, and thank me on your knees for making such excellent use of it. I do indeed, my adorable Mamma!

Such was the scene between us; but what pen can describe what I felt when at every turn of my head I beheld an angel in the person of my flagellator, whose every stroke, till nature ebbed away, transported me to regions of boundless felicity?

I know a young married couple that have always separate beds in the summer. Every morning the lady appears at breakfast in an elegant deshabille, and a most enormous bouquet on the left side of her bosom just fresh picked. When breakfast is over she retires to her bed-chamber, where her husband, dressed in his uniform (for he is an officer), soon follows her, and enjoys her *en levrette,* as they prefer that attitude as most voluptuous and favourable for conception. She says that her pleasure is more exalted from the sweet perfume of the bouquet, which she is constantly smelling to during the amorous engagement. She is particularly fond of the smell of wall-flowers. No married people I think live more happy, or have more beautiful children. Being one day on a visit at their country-house, her husband brought her from the garden a nosegay made of bunches of lilies of the valley, hyacinths, jonquils, minionet, auriculas, double wall-flowers, and violets, intermixed with sprigs of narrow myrtle in blossom, orange leaves, and sweet briar. All the sweet flowers the spring affords were united in the most beautiful bouquet I ever saw for the time of the year. She immediately pinned it to her bosom on the left side, and asked her husband how he liked her with it. He answered with a kiss; and, indeed, she looked so tempting and so effeminate, that I longed to give her another. She is not above nineteen; tall, rather slender, excessively fair a bosom — could I snatch the pencil of Correggio to give you an idea of it! — her hands and arms were symmetry itself. In the south of Europe nothing is more common than for Ladies to wear large nosegays, which occasions many Ladies in this country, I am positively sure, to do the same; indeed, when they go to public places they should wear them for many reasons. When I was in France I seldom saw a

Lady well dressed without one; the Countess Du Barry, of whipping memory, was never without one as large as a broom, the late King of France being excessively fond of them. I have been told that the present Queen of France, being subject to the head-ache, forbade them at Court for some time; but now this fashion is followed more than ever, as the Queen is grown fond of them. Though flowers have a most luxurious, nay salacious odour in the day time, yet one should be very careful not to sleep in a room with much of them, for the exhalation from them is very dangerous, especially in small bed-rooms. A young Lady that generally received the embraces of her husband in bed in a slight deshabille he was very fond of, and used to wear with it (as the lady above mentioned) a monstrous nosegay, one night forgetting to take it from her bosom after the amorous conflict, and being rather tired, fell asleep with it; in the morning she found herself very ill, and continued so for many days.

In my opinion a play on this subject would be vastly entertaining, supposing the principal characters to be Lady Birch, Lady Tickletail, Mrs. Flogwell, Mrs. Ticklebum, Lady Bouquet, Signora Birchini, Miss Blossom, the three last fond of whipping with enormous bouquets in their bosoms, Mademoiselle Dubouleau, the Governess, and Lord Frolicksome, Lord Frisky, Sir H. Prancer, Lord Jessamy, a few boys and girls, as Miss Giddy, Miss Tomboy, &c.

T A L E S

Translated from the F R E N C H.

It is necessary to be observed, that the character by whom those Tales are related, is supposed to posses the peculiar intuitive advantages of an invisible spy.

TALE THE FIRST.

ONE evening as I sat in pensive melancholy in my chamber, entered a sweet little tit, attired in all the charms of tempting deshabille, heightened by a swelling bosom, adorned by a well selected nosegay, and a little after her, a young fellow of the sprightly age of between twenty and thirty years

The doors being carefully shut, the curtains drawn, and every crevice secured with the utmost caution, the girl addressed him in an authoritative tone, to this effect — Well, abandoned wretch, whence came you? Did not I charge you not to go out without my leave? My dear mother, returned the young man, in the most submissive tone, indicating all the tremour of a school-boy, I am come from catechism. From catechism impudence at this hour, said the mistress, you tell me a lye, accompanying the reproof with two or three blows on the ear, and as many kicks on the breech. Let me see, let me see, says she, what you have learned. How many mortal sins are there? There are, — there are, — my dear mother — I cannot exactly remember how many there are. — What, sirrah, do you not remember your mortal sins? O then I'll learn you to remember them. Come, Sir, strip, strip this instant. My dear mother, cried the culprit, pray forgive me; I will learn them. No, no, replied the other, snatching a bundle of rods, you shall be whipt; strip, strip I say. With that she unbuttoned his small clothes, pulled them down to the knees, and tucked his shirt up above his shoulders. When he had received about half-a-dozen stripes, he pretended to ward them off with his hands, but she tied them before him, and plied the birch till the blood flowed most copiously.

What now could mortal imagine would be the consequence? Why the scene was immediately changed: the scholar became master and the mistress became scholar, and underwent a severe flogging in her turn; and there is not a doubt but the parties received a mutual and most exquisite pleasure.

These means, said I to myself, though singular and comical, have a powerful effect in stimulating the generative faculties. Singular and comical, replied a genius at my elbow; nothing is more natural or fashionable at present. It is a ceremony used in all the temples consecrated to Venus, which are always provided with a good stock of birch for the accommodation of their votaries, as an excellent means for putting the blood in motion. Ladies of taste always take care to have a bundle of well-seasoned rods under their bolsters for their own use or that of their paramour. It is an infallible nostrum to invigorate nature, enliven cold constitutions, and we are told by the faculty that it is a sovereign remedy in cases of sterility. A wag then remarked that the hand of a lusty knave of a Friar could never afford such exquisite sensation as that of a pretty woman, and that therefore the devotees to the sex would become easily habituated to the chastisement of the young and mettlesome sisterhood: so much for this ceremony and its extraordinary effects.

TALE THE SECOND.

An unfortunate fair one being enjoined by a reverend father to do penance for the operation of an enormous offence, by receiving fifty stripes with the rod, the necessary preparations were made for the solemn occasion.

The poor delinquent confessing her crime, with blushes, tucked up, and submitted her posteriors to the mercy of the old castigator, who, provided with an excellent implement of green birch, laid on without ceremony. These churchmen, said a female auditor, are surely without pity. That's very true, replied one of the other sex, hardness of heart is their just reproach, but under such circumstances a man of the world would have been as little susceptible of pity. The culprit was beautiful, had a skin of the lily whiteness, and had scarcely reached to enchanting fifteen. Such rapturous charms are too affecting to the view to admit of dispensing with an opportunity for admiring them, and as that could not be afforded with decency, but on the occasion of inflicting punishment, the good father seemed in no hurry to put an end to it, though the posteriors and thighs streamed with blood.

The poor girl bore the correction with all possible resignation, and the good father exercised the discipline with all the alacrity as could become so wholesome an institution.

TALE THE THIRD.

In early life I was apprentice to a school-mistress, a most unmerciful dispenser of the birch, who upon a certain occasion placed me in a closet, near the schoolroom, where the larger girls were commonly corrected, so that I had an opportunity of seeing almost every day, to my most exquisite pleasure, perhaps a dozen of the most beautiful pictures.

My mistress had, besides two under tutoresses, a niece who carried as much authority as herself in the school, and, after her example, spared the posteriors of the poor girls as little; indeed, flagellation seemed to be her darling passion. She was about twenty, tall, well proportioned, always attired in becoming taste, and seldom without a large nosegay on one side of her bosom, for she encouraged the fashion of wearing enormous nosegays by her own example. The smallest faults were punished with whipping — thirty well applied stripes were the ordinary correction. Sometimes this lady, who always corrected the larger girls, from twelve to fourteen years of age, stretched the punishment to fifty stripes, with rods of green birch.

The purveyor who supplied this school had particular orders to send no brooms but such as were composed of birch newly cut; for this experienced matron well knew that the dry birch had a tendency to discolour the skin too much. Some seemed to receive the chastisement without concern, and affected levity as much after as before the discipline, whilst others expressed their feelings by the bitterest cries, and endeavoured to ward off the stripes with their hands; but all in vain, for instead of obtaining any degree of favour, their hands were tied before them, and they received a double number of stripes.

Notwithstanding this severity of correction, the school was very full, as the greatest part of female parents approve of such rigorous discipline; and, indeed, it must be acknowledged, that punishment was never inflicted without desert. A number of very beautiful ladies came out of this school as accomplished and deeply skilled in Birch discipline as any from out of a convent.

A-pro-pos, replied a lady, who had been educated in a convent, don't you imagine that the tenants of the cloistered domains are of so delicate a texture, they well know the virtues of the birch, and so frequent is the practice of flagellation there, that it will be difficult to equal them in the exercise of the art.

It was at length confessed that this method of castigation was of infinite service to young girls, who thought themselves women before their time, and, after having spent five or six years at these schools, came out of them as uninformed as they went in. One day the niece came into the closet set apart for correction, and began to make a bundle of rods from a new broom which the servant maid brought her. She then called in a young girl of about thirteen or fourteen years of age, who immediately on the sight of the rods began to cry, and ask pardon. A truce to your tears, cried the other; you know what I promised you this morning, you must be whipt; upon which she pulled up her petticoats and shifts as high as she could, put her head under her left arm, and holding her fast in this position, the buttocks and thighs being well exposed, she began to apply the birch. I'll do so no more, cried the poor delinquent. You shall have it, says the other, proceeding in the discipline, her eyes indicating the pleasure it afforded, till having glutted her humour by exciting a profusion of blood, she threw down the rod, and reclined on a chair almost breathless. This passion, it was added, prevails with the women in general, from the school-mistress to the mistresses of the different arts and professions, of which the narrator declares himself to be perfectly assured.

For the SECOND PART of the FEMALE FLAGELLANTS.

Miss C——h, when she bore that name, took under her care the two daughters of an officer in the Guards, whose wife had been her intimate companion, and was lately deceased. They were both remarkably beautiful, fair and plump of their age — one thirteen, the other turned of fourteen. She dressed them always in the highest elegance and wantonness; had them taught every accomplishment under her own eye, and always corrected every fault with the birch, and with her own hand. She had a confidant in the late L——y H——, who was remarkably fond of assisting and seeing such exhibition. She used to send for her on these occasions; and her woman, from whom I had these particulars, assured me they would be sometimes an hour before they would let their coats down. They used to place their two chairs in a line, and one lay up one girl, and the other the other, with their posteriors over against each other, so as to have a view of both at once, then they used to whip them a little, and then compare their ivory globes, and then whip them again alternately, but never severely. And the same person told me the girls grew so fond of it, that they have often begged her in the most earnest manner to take them up at other times, which she says she frequently did, and used to take it from them again herself.

WHIMSICAL ANECDOTE.

A certain E—— has two beautiful young daughters, Lady M—— and Lady H——, the former twelve, the latter eleven years of age. There was a handsome little boy, of nine years of age, who attended Lady M—— as her foot boy. With him the young Ladies used to play many innocent tricks, and to pass many jokes upon him. One very extraordinary joke we must not omit recording. They had persuaded him to believe that he must implicitly comply with, and perform, whatever they should be pleased to order and direct, otherwise he would lose his place, by being immediately turned off with shame and disgrace; upon which he declared that he should at all times be ready, as was his duty, to obey and fulfil their Ladyships' orders and commands as far as lay in his power. Upon this declaration the young Ladies dismissed Tom (that being his name) for the present, with orders to knock softly at their bed-chamber door next morning at eight o'clock. Tom was punctual in obeying this command, and obtained immediate admittance. The young Ladies received him in their shifts, and made him follow them into their closet. As soon as they entered they shut the door, upon which Lady M—— got up upon a chair, and stood upon it with her posteriors bared, having pulled up her smock for that purpose, while Lady H—— ordered the little submissive lackey to kneel down at the foot of the chair, and to kiss Lady M——'s *noble* parts repeatedly, and to be very careful not to let the *proper* place miss his fervent embraces. When Lady M—— had *indulged* him as long as she thought proper, she descended, and was succeeded by her sister, Lady H——, who mounted the chair, and uncovered her bumfiddle, in the same manner that Lady M—— had done, upon which the particoloured urchin was commanded to kneel a second time, and to impress his embraces in the same *luxuriant* manner he had done to Lady M——; which he did with a degree of unaccountable and extraordinary ecstasy on the beautiful posteriors of both the divine and angelic sisters. When these most charming young Ladies had amused themselves as long as they thought proper with their little slave, whom they had made most happy by their confidence they dismissed him with an injunction to return next morning at the same hour, and not to impart to any one, on no account whatever, the use or purpose to which they had applied him; all which commands he promised most faithfully to adhere to. This kind of commerce Lady M—— and Lady H—— carried on with their *favourite* Tom for about three weeks, when a quarrel happened between Dick (Lady H——'s foot-boy) and Tom; in the course of which Dick told him, that although their Ladies admitted him (Tom) into their bed-chamber, he was determined not to be ill-used by him. Lady H——'s maid, who happened to be present at this dispute, was determined to avail herself of the truth of Dick's assertion. She accordingly watched Tom, and saw him admitted next morning into the young Ladies' bed-chamber, upon which she applied her eye to the key-hole, but could only see them retire to the adjoining closet, through which she pierced a small opening, and beheld, with much surprise, Lady M—— and Lady H——, with Tom prostrate, as above related. She immediately informed the young Ladies' Governess of what she had seen, who went to their apartment, and discovered them exhibiting in the *luscious* scene, agreeable to their peculiar and singular *penchant*. The Governess acquainted the Countess, their step-mother, of the whole affair, who was all astonishment at the relation, and immediately commanded the young culprits into her presence, whom she rated very severely for a considerable time. Her Ladyship then ordered her maid, who was in waiting, to go to the shrubbery and bring her a very good rod, for the purpose of whipping very heartily the backsides of those audacious, impudent young hussies. The rod being brought, the young Ladies immediately fell on their knees, imploring their dear Mamma's forgiveness, and promising never to offend again; but all to no purpose, for her Ladyship, after seating herself upon the sopha, ordered the Governess to bring Lady M—— to her, whom she laid across her knee: having exposed her *lovely* backside to the rod, she whipped her soundly for full five minutes, and afterwards exerted herself on the *beautiful* posteriors of her charming sister.

Still these young wantons were not terrified from such salacious amusement — for about a fortnight after, they feigned a slight sickness, for the pleasure of lying in bed, and were caught by their mother making use of an indiscreet toy. The Lady was enraged to frenzy on beholding such a scene; but stifled her rage till she returned with an excellent rod. The writer of these anecdotes happened to be on a visit, and could not conceive what the Lady was at when she saw her leave the room with the birchen sceptre, till, hearing the cries of her daughters, she ran upstairs, and discovered the exasperated Lady holding the culprits down in bed, and whipping them with the utmost severity.

What surprised the writer very much was to see two full grown girls kicking and plunging under the heavy strokes of the rod, and suffering their delightful posteriors to be left in the condition of a schoolboy after a whipping from a savage schoolmaster, when their united strength could vanquish their mother. But it seems whenever they made resistance, the Lady tied them alternately with a belt down on a chair, and whipped them without mercy.

For the SECOND PART of the FEMALE FLAGELLANTS.

The Editor of the Female Flagellants, in the Note, page 31, says that she is informed that Birch discipline is never used in any boarding-school, *meaning for young Ladies.*

This information is wrong.

There are *some* schools, *in and near* Town, where the rod is never applied; but in many the pupils are obliged to undergo the Birchen correction whenever they are detected in a fault, sometimes even for a very trivial one. In the girls' schools in the great Towns, at a distance from London — such as Litchfield, Exeter, Salisbury, and Worcester, whither children are often sent from hence, the use of the rod is as common as at the Public schools for boys. The mistresses and tutoresses whip their scholars, big girls as well as little ones, without any scruple. They are either horsed on the back of a big girl or obliged to lie down on a stool — just as the Lady who flogs finds convenient. In most schools some girl has her learning and board gratis, to perform the services of sweeping the school, making the rods, and holding up the young Ladies to be whipt. At most of these schools a Writing-master attends to teach the scholars, and I have known several times, when a Mistress has detected a naughty Miss in a very flagrant offence, such as persisting in a fib, stealing from her fellow scholars, *telling tales out of school*, &c., she has thought herself not equal to the task of giving the proper punishment, and has employed the Writing-master to inflict it upon girls of thirteen or fourteen years of age. When this happens poor Miss's backside smarts severely, as Master lays on the rod with a heavy hand, so as to mark the culprit with the signs of the lash, from the top of her buttocks down to her garters, while the Mistress and the Tutoresses, and perhaps a Birch loving Lady besides, sit by, and enjoy the twistings and postures of the beautiful little sufferer. Some parents don't mind these things, and others never hear of it, as the girls are afraid to tell, no crime being so severely corrected as telling tales out of school. I have observed that young Ladies who are orphans, or whose friends live at a great distance, as in the West Indies, or Ireland, are frequently whipped for faults which others escape correction for; and as no letter goes from school without being examined, if any attempt is made to complain by writing, Miss must expect to be horsed and flogged without mercy, until her backside is almost flayed, and this would be done before all the scholars as an example of what they are to expect if they say anything of their sufferings. Ladies don't like to own these facts, but I know them to be true, and many have owned to me, after they have left school, that all this is true. I have seen swinging Birch rods at many girls' schools. Some Mistresses and Masters make the poor little things kiss the rod every time they are whipped.

I am,

Your humble Servant,

VAPULATOR.

March 22,
1785.

To the EDITOR of the SECOND PART of the
FEMALE FLAGELLANTS.

MADAM,

Amidst a number of curious anecdotes, permit me to introduce one as singular, and, perhaps, of more benefit to the world at large.

Chatting with a select party of my female friends last night, and running over many striking particulars in the Fashionable Lectures, and the first part of your work, a lady, after hearing many observations on the subject of whipping, introduced an anecdote that may be of infinite service to many whose lives are made miserable through the want of children.

A few years ago she formed an intimacy with a young couple of good fortune, who had been married some years without being blest with a child. The woman was beautiful, and wore a prolific appearance, and the husband seemed as able a General as ever acquired laurels in the fields of Venus.

What with the sneers of the ill-natured, and the jests of friends, the gentleman had but a sore time of it. And this would have continued for some years longer, in all probability, had not a lady made her appearance in the family, who had just arrived from a convent in France.

This lady was sister to the sterile lady, and loved her as her life; nor was she a whit less fond of the husband, who was her relation, and had been her play-mate when a boy.

Hearing him severely roasted one evening about his wife's sterility, she, on her return home, told them both if they would suffer her to administer a remedy she would forfeit her life if she did not succeed. This remedy a well informed lady in France communicated to her, with an assurance of its certain success.

When she mentioned the particulars they laughed immoderately, but they were so anxious to possess a child, with her earnest entreaties, they complied. The lady of the house instantly sent for a new broom, out of which she desired the maid to make a large rod for her dog, and bring it to her. While this was settling the sister dressed herself as splendid as possible in the French taste, and, having got the rod from the servant, and tied those twigs together she liked best, she entered her sister's chamber in a great passion, where she and her husband were enfolded in each other's arms. When the lady found everything right between the couple, she instantly pulled the gentleman's breeches down to his heels, and having tucked in his shirt above his waist, she plied the rod gently, upbraiding him the whole time (as was agreed between them) about his inactivity in not getting his wife with child — the language between them running in something like the following strain:—

The L E C T U R E.

Will you for ever, you great lazy rascal, expose your wife and yourself to the derision of every one? will you, will you, will, will, will, will you, you impotent young scoundrel? "Oh, no, my dear, lovely sister, I will not indeed! I will not, upon my honour!" I'll make you, you shall not! I am determined to put life into you now, and not call a blush eternally into my sister's face and your own! yes, yes, yes, yes, yes, yes, yes, yes, you shall learn activity from this excellent rod before I have done, you may rest assured! "Oh, my dear sister! Oh, my dear, dear, beautiful sister, for God's sake, don't whip so hard! I promise you you shall not have this fault to complain of any more! Charlotte, my dear, angelic Charlotte, lay aside the rod!" I will not lay aside the rod, I will not, upon my honour, till I make you as active and sprightly as any husband existing! Keep him down, my dear sister; don't let him get away till I am satisfied he will do as I would have him! — I knew another lazy gentleman in France, whose wife could get no good of him till a good rod was as well applied to his backside as this I exercise now! "Charlotte! Charlotte! my dearest, lovely Charlotte! my adorable Charlotte, let me go!" — You shall not go; hold him, sister, hold him tight! He shall find it not an easy matter to get from under the rod when I take it in hand! yes, yes, I see how active you can be when a good rod is well applied; your motions are brisk enough now! You may take my word for it you shall feel it often while I remain in this house! "Oh, Charlotte! Charlotte! my sweet sister! my lovely Charlotte, I — die — with — trans — port!" In that moment she threw her arm over his back and whipt him smartly, till he gained the summit of his felicity.

It may appear strange, but it is a fact, that in one of the three whippings he got in this manner, his wife conceived, and in about nine months after they were blest with a lovely boy, and Charlotte, for her assistance, had an elegant present of diamonds at his birth.

The lady said she knew the flagellating lady very intimately, and declared, when drest, no woman could look lovelier. She declared to the lady who related the anecdote, from what she had heard on the Continent, she was satisfied the splendour of the flagellator's dress heightens the bliss in a supreme degree; and she altered her dress each time as much as she possibly could, that he might fancy her a new character, or one that had charmed him in the course of his walks that day.

Yours, &c.,

CHARLOTTE.

Bristol, March 17, 1785.

P.S. — *I think a good metzotinto print from this anecdote would be very highly prized by the lovers of fine women and birch.* — *Should any of your readers wish to know why a whipping from a female hand should give birth to conception, that learned and pleasing treatise on flogging the loins and reins, by* Dr. Meibomius, *will satisfy them.*

For the SECOND PART of the FEMALE
FLAGELLANTS.

Bath, March 3, 1785.

Madam,

The first part of your work excited my curiosity very
much; indeed, so strongly was I pressed to read it, that I
solicited a female friend who was just setting out for
London to send it by the first conveyance.

Many of the anecdotes are whimsical to a degree, and
I must say prettily put together. I have read them, and
heard them read, in many a private party, and do assure
you, though many of them do not wear a face of
probability, yet the Ladies, one and all, declared them in
a great measure faithful pictures of whipping pastime.

I am not, I assure you, fond of feeling the rod, even
from the hand of a Goddess, having had enough of it
while under the tuition of a Governess as merciless as
she was ugly. But to the point.

Reading the story of Mrs. E—— this morning to my
maid as she was dressing me, and expressing somewhat
of surprise at such a passion in women, she assured me
the following anecdote was in every point authentic:—

A Lady, with whom she lived formerly, was so devoted to the pleasure, that she set two days of every week apart for enjoying it. A whipping from the hands of a Lady of equal years she delighted highly in, but to be well whipt by a full grown girl transported her. She had a sister equally fond of it, who lived with her, and who, with my maid, were the only persons in the secret.

This Lady happened to spend a few weeks at Buxton Wells, where she formed an intimacy with a family of distinction, consisting of a gentleman, his two daughters, and his sister, who took care of the girls, their mother being dead. The eldest of these girls was the finest picture of true beauty ever seen, and her vivacity was equal to her beauty. At this period she was fourteen years old, all life and spirits, and the soul of every company she entered into.

The Lady saw and adored; but how to gain the summit of her felicity was the question.

Miss N. was highly delighted with the company of the Lady, who we may suppose exerted herself to the highest degree to rivet the affections of her blooming charmer. The maid set her wits to work, and as Abigails are fertile at expedients, she succeeded.

It was fixed that the young Ladies should be invited, without the aunt, to spend a day with the two Ladies. They came, and all was mirth and hilarity; they romped, tickled, and diverted themselves with a number of innocent pranks, till at length the Lady turned up Miss's clothes and gave her a few gentle slaps, observing at the same time how happy she should be to be her Governess, for the pleasure of tickling her pretty backside.

Miss took it all in jest, and laughed over it with great glee; after which the Lady's sister whispered Miss N—, and they retired for a few minutes. Now this was the very thing the Abigail had concerted. In a little while the Ladies returned to the parlour, Miss with a rod in her hand, and the Lady's sister recommending her to make a proper use of it, and offering her assistance to hold the Lady.

The instant the Lady saw them enter, she made an effort to seize the rod, but was instantly overpowered by her sister and the two Misses, who all compelled her to lie on a small table, and suffer herself to be whipt by her young Mamma. The other young Lady seeing her kick, got under the table, and, lying flat on her belly, held the culprit's legs, while she seemed to endeavour, by pulling up her petticoats, slapping her little bum, and other efforts, to disengage her limbs from her; all which, as she wished no doubt, proved ineffectual, nor would the Lady's sister, who held her down the whole time, suffer the pretty flagellator to leave off till she thought the Lady was transported, which did not happen to be the case, till her posteriors wore the stripes generally seen on those from the hands of a flagellating step-mother, or a severe French Governess. As soon as the Lady got up, she laughed immoderately, and throwing her arms round the neck of her disciplinarian, kissed her with ecstasy, and told her she would make an admirable Governess. Miss laughed at the observation, and told her it was her sister's doings entirely, who called her out and insisted on it, observing at the same time how pleased she would be to assist me, and she was certain you would take it all in good part. So I do, upon my honour, said the Lady, kissing her lovely hand, and the only retaliation I require is that you inflict the same punishment on my sister this minute. The sister made an attempt to get away, but the Lady took care to hold her down, till Miss exercised the rod with bewitching severity. Thus were they both delighted, nor did Miss know a little about the truth of the matter the whole time.

To the PUBLISHER of the FEMALE FLAGELLANTS.

Sir,

Laughing some time ago with a party of lively girls of the Cyprian train, over a print representing a number of boarding-school girls going to flagellate the governess, one of the ladies related an anecdote as whimsical as any I have yet read or heard, which is much at your service, either to insert in the second part of the Female Flagellants, or to stimulate you to take your pencil in hand and make two good paintings from it.

Belinda (for such is the Lady's name who related the anecdote) was placed out, at a very early age, at a boarding school, a few miles from town, under the tuition of a woman who possessed the most insinuating address in the female world, which always secured her a sufficient number of pupils — having through it acquired a great name among parents and guardians.

A short while after Belinda had been at school, the Governess turned off her assistant; and, seeing an advertisement in the Morning Post from a French tutoress, she sent for her and instantly engaged her. This, said Belinda, we all set down as a high proof of her taste, as the lady, who was a native of Picardy, was one of the most charming women in the world. Her stature was majestic, but her air and demeanour was nature itself. The peculiar splendour of her carriage was softened and subdued by the most affable condescension — her charms inspired universal rapture! The softest roses that ever youth and modesty poured out on beauty glowed on the lip of this lovely woman. Her cheeks were the bloom of Hebe, and all that could transport human nature adorned her swelling bosom. This flight of ecstasy, said Belinda, ran from one girl to another through the school on her appearance, little suspecting what a flagellating spirit lurked beneath this fascinating exterior.

Madame Whipperanti (a name, said Belinda, we baptized her by a short while after she made her appearance) was not above two days in the school when she addressed our governess in French, asking if she suffered the use of the rod in her school, to which she answered yes; because, said the French lady, I have observed no sign of any such useful implement since I entered your school.

I have had no occasion, said the governess, to take it in hand. Pardon me, said the other, you have been repeatedly provoked to it in my own hearing by three or four dunces: but you are too easy, madam. I never found any admonition produce so powerful an effect as a good birch-rod well handled; and I would forfeit my life, with the assistance of a good one, I would work such a reformation that you would be eased of one-half the burthen attending your present system of tuition.

This was said, said Belinda, in our hearing, and you may be certain we looked at each other, and at her with astonishment.

What with this advice in our hearing and enforcing it in private, backed by a niece to the governess, who was an assistant in the school, the lady, who we thought no bad hand before the arrival of Madame Whipperanti, gave into it at once, and it fell to my lot, said Belinda, to be the second whose posteriors were smartly whipped by this woman.

But the most laughable anecdote throughout this business is the following:—

This woman, anxious, I can safely swear, for a general display of backsides, dropped a little French book in a bed-room where about a dozen of the girls slept, in which many voluptuous scenes were described, illustrated with a number of prints of an inflammatory tendency.

Maria C——, who was the life and soul of our society, and who was a compleat mistress of French, translated the whole of the work, and set us cock-a-hoop to put in practice many of the scenes. One in particular struck our fancy, and seemed to give us a higher notion of the good things of this life than any other.

This was a print and glowing passage, where an amorous engagement with a mock —— is described. The belt and the machine were in a short while manufactured by the fertile genius of Maria, and we had, as soon as we had tasted the divine sweets flowing from it, above a dozen made in the course of a couple of days.

About a week had elapsed after this charming discovery, when one morning, which happened to be a holiday, Madame Whipperanti, wishing no doubt for a grand entertainment on the bumfiddle, watched our motions so very close, that she brought the Governess to a peep-hole she made in the next room, who observing how we were engaged — for we were all in high ecstasy, except Maria, whose belt gave way, and whose companion was fastening it on — the Governess, with her flagellating companion, Miss Harriet, the niece, and a lady who was a boarder in the family, all burst into the room, and threw our divine party into the greatest confusion. Some ran out of an opposite door, who were soon overtaken, and we were instantly guarded to the schoolroom. Nothing but birch and flaying of bums echoed around. The maids were ordered up stairs. Such as endeavoured to escape were tied down on chairs and stools. Some were horsed, who were not easily managed, among whom was your humble servant, who was mounted on the back of a maid-servant as powerful as an Hercules. Nothing was heard around but roaring, crying, the sound of the rods, and the most impassioned lectures.

I fancy to this hour, said Belinda, laughing, Madame Whipperanti took an uncommon liking to my posteriors, for I remember well she kept me up full five minutes, and exercised the rod with such severity, using very little intermission, that with all her beauties, from her brilliant eyes to her angelic hand and arm, and from that to her matchless leg and foot, I could not feel anything of transport in it; though I am well persuaded any of the male creation would have thought it next a journey to heaven to have felt her pull his breeches down, and tuck in his shirt above his waist with as much deliberation and seeming pleasure as she lifted my petticoats, and the rod exercised by her magic hand with the utmost vigour.

Indeed, I am convinced to this hour Madame Whipperanti had a violent liking for my bumfiddle, for I remember well while she was untying the instrument of pleasure, which was fastened round my middle, she complained of the knot, slapped my posteriors with her hand, and run it over both cheeks repeatedly, till she had disengaged the instrument. But this was not the only thing that convinced me of her love for my posterior beauties, for every time I turned my head to implore forgiveness during her exercising the rod, I could perceive her beautiful eyes ready to bounce out of her head — so lost was she in transport.

It was certainly the richest feast for a backside

voluptuary imaginable, to see such a number of bums in one view! I should say before the punishment, for after it they were sadly discoloured, no poor culprits having ever received a severer flagellation. Madame Whipperanti, I have been informed, lives now with a merchant of immense fortune in the city, who no doubt will bequeath her something considerable for the felicity he receives from her hands.

To the EDITOR of the EXHIBITION of FEMALE FLAGELLANTS.

Madam,

As I find you mean to publish a Second Part of the Female Flagellants, I send you the following anecdotes which have been lately communicated to me by a friend, and which (when corrected) might perhaps amuse many of your readers.

Yours,

CLARINDA.

Miss B—— was the daughter of a merchant, who, having suffered many losses, was obliged to become a bankrupt. As she was of a very amorous disposition, a most charming girl, with pretty blue eyes, always swimming in the fluid of amorous dalliance, it is no wonder if she fell a victim to the late Lord ——. Sir H. G., who had spent many years in Italy, and had tasted very often the felicity of a birch-rod from the hands of the Italian Ladies — who, as fame reports, are more expert at giving pleasure in that way than any women in Europe — meeting her one day at an exhibition, he joined her, and as he knew she was *comeatable*, he proposed to take her into keeping, which she accepted. He saw her home, dined with her, and soon after he introduced his favourite subject. She immediately understood him, but having no rod by her, she sent her maid for one to a Mantua-maker who lived in the same house, and who having a number of children and apprentices, was never without a good birch-rod. The maid soon returned with a most excellent one. After whipping and lecturing him for a considerable time, she found to her great surprise it had not the desired effect.

He proposed to her to go to Kensington, and ordered the coachman to stop at a nursery reputed for selling beautiful flowers, and furnishing the fair votaries to

Flora with handsome bouquets. He soon presented her with a most elegant one, and so excessively large, that she could scarcely pin it to her bosom. After a few turns in the garden they returned home. On entering her bedroom she found on the bed a new birch-rod, which the careful maid had provided during her absence. She took it up, and, assuming a severe look, she, in the character of an angry mother, whipped him as severely as she could, and so well acted her part, that he soon gave her proof of his being a very good boy. He owned to her afterwards that the sweet smell of flowers had always an uncommon effect on him; that when he was about ten years old, it was his delight to provoke his step-mother to whip him — she being a beauty of the first order, and not then above seventeen, excessively fond of flowers, and seldom without a monstrous bouquet in her bosom.

That, however, the flowers had not the least effect on him but when made in a nosegay, and placed on one side of the bosom of a pretty woman. Miss B—— knew very well the influence of flowers in men as well as in women (a knowledge, however, that few women possess); but as to whipping, she was rather a stranger to it. One day he told her it would give him the highest felicity to see her whip a young girl in some elegant dress. Miss B—— soon prevailed on the Mantua-maker to send her one of her daughters as a little companion — a bold little girl about eleven, as she was to teach her to read and work, by way of amusement. She soon found herself obliged to smart her bum with the birch-rod. A woman of Miss B——'s disposition could not but find a new source of amusement in that employment; and, indeed, she exercised the rod as often as she could.

However, wishing to gratify Sir H. G., she dressed one day in the most elegant manner, not forgetting to wear on one side of her bosom, quite up to her ear, a monstrous bouquet, or rather a broom, of the most odoriferous flowers! When the hour approached that she expected him, she made the girl read to her, slapping her hands now and then with a large rod made of new birch: and as soon as she heard him coming she retired with the girl to her bed-chamber — protesting she would whip well the little lazy slut; made her go on her knees, kiss the rod, &c.; then lifting her clothes to her middle, she began to whip her with all the severity of a school-mistress, throwing her in the most wanton attitudes; her pretty bosom heaving all the time with tumultuous joy, her eyes sparkling with ecstasy, and her pretty face partly buried in the nosegay! As there was a glass door, Sir H. G. could plainly see this luxurious scene, and was so highly pleased with it, that he settled a pretty annuity on her that very day.

A friend of mine who, a few years ago, resided at Edinburgh, was acquainted there with a Miss F——, a professed disciplinarian, who kept a genteel day-school for young Ladies. As she lived in the same house, she had been a witness to many curious whipping scenes. Miss F—— was then about twenty-five, a tall, handsome girl, carrying the passion of whipping to an extreme.

One day as my friend was at breakfast with her, a beautiful girl, about fourteen or fifteen, entered the parlour, and delivered into her hands, with a seemingly dejected air, a little note. After reading it, she told her to wait a minute, then running out of the parlour, she soon returned with a birch-broom. As she left the note on the table, my friend had the curiosity to read it — the contents of which were:— Mrs. S——'s compliments to Miss F——, will be for ever thankful to her, if she will take the trouble of giving her daughter a good whipping, having been very disrespectful to her this morning. She then ordered the girl to prepare herself for a good whipping. After making a shocking rod, she turned her petticoats as high as she could, pinned her smock to her shoulders; then holding her tight under her left arm, she began to whip her so severely, that in a minute her beautiful bum was crimsoned as deep as the finest rose. O, Miss, forgive me, for God's sake! cried the young girl — I can't bear it! no, no, no, no ! I shan't, till I have left a sample of this excellent birch on your pretty bottom! Will you ever disoblige your mother — will, will, will, will, will you! No, no, indeed. Ma'am, I assure you I never will! To say I should be obliged to whip a girl almost fit to be married; but, indeed, Mr. Birch is the only husband fit for a bold girl like you! How do you like him? — tell, tell, tell, tell, tell, is he not a sweet man?

After whipping her for full five minutes, seeing her a—e and thighs in weals, she gave over; but to shame her the more, she stuck in her bosom a monstrous bundle of birch.

About half a-year after, as my friend was walking about the Castle, she saw two young Ladies elegantly dressed — one resembling so much the girl she had seen whipt, that she drew near her in order to satisfy herself, and found it was the same. She accosted her, and found by her conversation she had been lately married. Nothing could equal the elegance of her dress: instead of a bundle of birch, she wore, as well as her fair companion, an enormous side bouquet of natural flowers, with a black hat full of large white feathers. As soon as she went home, she told Miss F—— who she had seen; who, far from being surprised, told her that nothing was more common in Scotland than for girls to marry at that age — that she had whipped some a week before they were married; that the young Lady in question had been married to a rich merchant, a widower, with a boy of ten, and a girl of nine years old.

Curious to know how this young Lady behaved to her step-children, my friend contrived to become intimate with her. One day she was on a visit at her house, the children behaved very undutiful to her, which exasperated her so much, that she rung the bell and ordered her maid to get her a good birch-rod. You know, Ma'am, said she, how Miss F—— served me not long ago; if you will excuse me, I will serve these bold children in the same manner. By all means, said my friend; I think they deserve a good whipping. The maid soon brought her an excellent rod. She took hold immediately of the boy, and, pulling his breeches to his heels, she whipped him till she was tired. After resting a few minutes, she took the girl and served her just like the boy.

As my friend was on a very intimate footing with her, she made her confess that she was not only excessively fond of whipping, but delighted in being herself whipt, though not altogether so severely as Miss F—— used to whip her scholars; that her husband was as great a votary to birch-discipline as herself, and she generally whipped him every night before they went to bed. That she had prevailed on a cousin of hers, a girl about her age and of the same humour, to come sometimes to help her to whip her husband, when they would dress in the most elegant manner, each with a bouquet of a monstrous size in their bosom; that her cousin, who generally was dressed like a school girl, would then whip him whilst he was engaged with her in the amorous combat.

Being one day, before her marriage, at his house, and seeing his children behaving very rudely, she said in joke, if she was their mother she would whip them well with a good birch-rod; upon which he sent the children out of the room, and throwing himself at her feet, begged she would accept of his hand, and take the care of his children upon her, but above all not to spare the rod. On recovering herself she told him if her mother would consent she had no objection: being a great match the mother consented immediately. She said she liked him very well, for though he had two children he was not thirty, having been married very young. He settled his whole fortune on her and her pretty cousin, a brother of his having left a considerable fortune to his children.

A doctor of my acquaintance told me he knew a girl about thirteen who was in a consumption, and almost given over. On the death of her mother she was sent to an aunt who lived in the North, where she recovered her health so well that in a couple of years she was as strong and healthy as any girl of her age. But what is very extraordinary, he attributed her recovery to the frequent whippings she got from her aunt.

This Lady had a numerous family, and was ignorant of the true situation of her niece, as the girl had been very much indulged during her mother's life, and that even her bad state of health had been attributed to that extreme indulgence and carefulness that prevails so much in some families; she would scarcely do anything she was bid. Her aunt, who was a proud, imperious woman, and used to whip her refractory children with the birch-rod with the utmost severity, soon served Miss in the same manner; would send her out to play in the garden with her children in the coldest weather, allowing her nothing but coarse wholesome food. In short, this girl is now married, has many children, and had she lived a little longer with her mother in all probability would be dead now.

This gentleman assured me he had recommended very often to several Ladies to punish with birch discipline their children when committing faults which appear to proceed from an heavy, bold, and indolent disposition, as nothing promotes the circulation of the blood better than a good rod, especially when made of new birch, and well applied to the posteriors — free, however, from cruelty.

To the PUBLISHER of the FEMALE FLAGELLANTS.

SIR,

I think the following lines merit a place in your curious repository of anecdotes in the Flagellant world.

Yours,

G. R.

AN ODE.

To Miss L——y W——n.

A beautiful girl, on finding her in tears, on having received, just before from her mother, the severe discipline of a birch-rod for a small transgression, though fourteen years of age.

> My charming Lydy, tell me why
> That blubber'd face, that wat'ry eye?
> Whom whilesome like a lambkin gay
> I saw so wanton, skip and play.
>
> Is little beau, thy goldfinch, flown?
> Or playsome kitten sulky grown?
> Has frolic squirrel broke his chain.
> And been sad author of thy pain?

Has saucy Tommy snatch'd a kiss,
Or done still something more amiss?
Has he through key-hole chanc'd to spy
Thy taper leg, or milk-white thigh?

These would not make my fair one grieve,
Nor her of wonted smiles bereave:
Far sharper evils cause her gloom,
A *Rod* has been poor Lydy's doom.

In vain at Mamma's feet she knelt,
Not less the tingling *Birch* she felt:
How hard, Mamma, must be thy heart
To make that lovely *Bum* to smart!

Bum, fairer far than Hebe's cheek!
Bum, more than Venny's bosom sleek!
Bum, than Ermine's down more white!
Bum, more than dazzling to the sight!

Those twinful orbs late spotless show,
Now with deep tints of crimson glow!
The blushing roses of her cheek,
Have rivals now not far to seek!

Hence, baleful twigs, from hence depart,
Curst *Birch* that caus'd my Lydy's smart;

May'st thou prove food for keenest fire,
And there, though late, thy stings expire!

Haste, little wanton, to my arms,
Intrust me with thy op'ning charms;
Let *me* now guard thee safe from *rods*,
And we'll be happier than the Gods!

To the EDITOR of the FEMALE FLAGELLANTS.

MADAM,

You seem to pay your whole attention to *modern* anecdotes, unmindful of what enraptured our ancestors. Pray, my dear Madam, did you never hear, or have you never read, that Queen Bess herself was most happy in the exercise of the rod, nay, that she gave transcendent felicity when she had a bold boy under correction? Methinks I see you open your eyes and wonder what is to follow; but do not be amazed, I will give you chapter and verse for my assertion.

The celebrated Earl of Essex, in one of the misunderstandings between him and Queen Elizabeth, having given her a more than common cause of offence, and wishing in a particular manner to soothe her resentment, wrote to her in the following terms. He gave the Queen, as we find in *Camden*, explicit thanks for the corrections she had inflicted upon him, and kissed (to use his words as recited by the above author), and *kissed her Majesty's Royal hand, and the rod which had chastised him.*

Now whether this Royal Disciplinarian figured in the character of a step-mother, a governess, or any other character remarked for the exercise of the rod, or whether she did it to please herself, or her noble admirer, matters not; it is certain she gave unbounded felicity when she took the rod in hand, if we credit his Lordship's assertion.

Indeed Queen Elizabeth is not the only great woman who has given pleasure with the rod, for we find the following anecdote in the Count of Bussi's *amorous history of Gauls*, a book which caused the disgrace of its author, on account of the liberties he had taken in it with the character of King Louis the Fourteenth, and his mistress *Madame de la Valiere*. The illustrious Count of Guiche, one of the first-rate beaus of the court of the King just mentioned, having committed a fault with the well-known Countess of Olonne, he wrote the next day to the Countess in the following words — "If you want me to die, I will bring you my sword; if you think I only deserve to be flagellated, I will come to you in my shirt."

I am equally astonished, Madam, that you have taken no notice of these gentlemen who are so passionately fond of a Lady's posterior beauties. I have heard of a gentleman who would kneel down, and, with the highest transport, ravish kisses from the posteriors of his mistress, and continue in that ecstasy above an hour.

Of these gentlemen who worship a Lady's bum with such enthusiastic rapture, and who have said and sung many pretty things about it, perhaps the following description from a pleasing French tale, entitled Araminta's Bumfiddle, will be found to approach the sublime nearer than any other on the subject.

Description of ARAMINTA's BUMFIDDLE.

By T I M A N T E.

I never was so taken with anything since I was born, Madam, as I was a little while ago with — you know what. Indeed, take it altogether, for beauty and good qualities, I do not believe there is the fellow of it upon the face of the earth: so plump! so smooth! so well proportioned! — And then for a complexion, that is to say, for a pure red and white! all the roses and lilies, the snow and vermillion that ever were bestowed upon Ladies' cheeks in sonnets and romances, from the beginning of the world to the date hereof, are nothing to it! And all this without the expense of pocket glasses, powders, paint, or patches; only an innocent wash now and then, and that is all. It is as true the pretty creature is as blind as Cupid, but then it is as sure to wound: and if it has no eyes, neither does it want any: because it has nothing to do but what may be done in the dark as well as in the light: and then the discretion of it is admirable. It is very sparing of speech; it has the wit never to refuse a good thing when it is offered, and tells no tales out of school when it has done. It is the common reconciler and rendezvous to both fools and philosophers; and, in one word, the support, the comfort, and the business of human nature.

More might be said *pro* and *con* in the case; but this shall suffice. My humble service, I beseech you, Madam, when you see my noble friend next. I know you may do me a good office there if you please; and I am sure you will, if you have that kindness for me, which I wish you may have, especially when you shall find that this gaiety of humour has in the bottom of it the highest degree of passion and respect that can enter into the soul of

TIMANTE.

Of these Ladies who have charmed with the magic exercise of the rod one anecdote deserves particular mention. The Lady who furnished the Publisher with the particulars has his thanks, hoping at the same time she will not be offended at seeing an abridgment of her letter, which, from the many repetitions in the Lecture, would be too heavy and unentertaining if the whole was printed.

Louisa Ticklebum (for so the Lady shall be called), when very young, was placed under the tuition of a Lady who kept a small boarding-school near Hyde-park corner. No woman in the universe ever took more pleasure than this Governess in whipping the bums of her little pupils, and no woman ever invented such modes of horsing the culprits. One way in particular she invented, that was in general use when she had a full-grown girl under the rod, which was a scale suspended from the centre of the room, the cord from which ran through two pullies, and was fastened in a corner of the room. This cord was loosened by two of the stoutest girls, who let the scale down till the culprit was tied on it with a belt, and then raised it to that height the Governess desired. The Lady would then, if the posteriors pleased her, keep the culprit up five minutes, and very often double the time, lecturing and whipping.

Louisa has often declared she could never account for her partiality to feeling and exercising the rod but through her being often severely whipped by this woman, who, though forty years old, to use the language of a celebrated writer, "Possessed the easiest and most elegant delivery, and accompanied her speech with the action of an arm of an exquisite form, and a hand as white as snow, and with a frown on her face which, without lessening its beauty, gave a true expression of her resentment." But the best picture of such a woman, at least the best I have ever seen, is that inimitable print of the Countess de Barre whipping the Marchioness de Rozen, which does distinguished honour to the designer and engraver; and here give me leave to introduce the anecdote in its genuine colours, for the print, to preserve beauty, is wide of the situation of the Marchioness when under the rod.

The Marchioness of Rozen, one of the attendants of the Countess of Provence, had for some time paid assiduous court to Madame de Barre. The latter liked her much; and they became intimate friends. The Marchioness was young and handsome, and had the air of a child. This observation is necessary. The Countess did not forget to invite her to a splendid entertainment. Madame de Rozen went, but shortly after broke off all connexion with her friend, or, at least, shewed a great coolness. This was probably owing to the Princess, whom she had the honour to serve, who had severely reproached her for her attention to a female so much the subject of public censure; and especially for her being noticed by the court as being present at her entertainments.

Whatever might have been the cause, the Countess was not insensible to the change. She complained to the King, who made a jest of the matter, saying, the Marchioness was but a child, for whom a rod was the fittest punishment. Madame de Barre took the King's words in the literal and most rigorous sense.

The Marchioness called on her one morning, and after they had breakfasted in a friendly manner together, the favourite invited her into her closet, as if she had something particular to tell her. That moment four lusty chambermaids seized upon the poor criminal, and whipt her soundly. The sufferer, boiling with rage, complained to the Sovereign, who had nothing to reply when the mistress reminded him that she had no more than executed the sentence of his Majesty.

He concluded with laughing at the affair; and Madame Rozen, by the advice of the Duke D'Aiguillon, revisited the Countess. After some raillery on the flagellated posteriors, which made known and confirmed the anecdote, the two friends embraced, and agreed to bury all in oblivion.

But to return to Louisa. — After she left school, she lived with her mother, a widow Lady, not a hundred miles from Chiswick. She had not been long at home before she had a general invitation to every family of consequence in the vicinity of that rural spot, and being a very fine girl, with a lively flow of conversation, she secured a number of admirers.

Notwithstanding all this, it so happened that she passed her four-and-twentieth year before any man thought seriously of marrying her. Indeed, the want of fortune was the chief reason for this neglect, and she would in all probability have remained longer without a bed-fellow if her exercise of the rod had not charmed a gentleman even to idolatry.

A Lady, sister to a merchant of London, spent a summer near her mother's, and took such a liking to Louisa, that she made her her bosom friend. Before they had been a month acquainted, they appeared like sisters, and nothing was pleasure with one that the other did not partake of. Louisa, in a frolic one day, when they were alone in a grotto, made a rod and proceeded to exercise it on her new friend, who was easily prevailed on to undergo the pleasing punishment, and from that day they seldom were alone without tasting this felicity. Indeed, they called in a third hand to partake of this pleasure, and that was a sister to the writer of these lines, who has often declared she took very high delight in this singular amusement.

Louisa was never so happy as when she had her loved friend on her lap, and her legs held by her other confidante, while she made her bold daughter's backside smart with the rod.

The merchant had often heard his sister mention Louisa in the highest strain of panegyric, and never longed more to accumulate a plumb than he did to see her. In a short while he beheld and adored! he raved of her morning, noon, and night! bumpered her whenever he sacrificed to Bacchus! and swore, by the bright Goddesses of Charles the Second's court, there never was a lovelier woman born. But what enraptured him most was her magic exercise of the rod.

The merchant was a widower, though not above five and thirty, and had an only child, a son, who was indulged in everything, and who was then about eight years old. Louisa took a great liking to the boy, and had him at her mother's above a month, when one Sunday, after her return from church, she was informed the boy had wantonly trampled on a bed of flowers she had taken great pleasure in raising. She was in a great passion, and scolded the child severely, when at the moment she beheld his father alight from his phaeton at the gate, who, on entering the parlour, seeing her features disturbed, pressed to know the cause. She told him the whole affair, adding with much warmth, if she had that dominion over the youth she wished for she would make his backside smart with a good rod. O! my dear Madam, said the Gentleman (his eyes bouncing out of his head at the sound), pray take a rod in hand this moment, and whip him well, for I assure you he never got a taste of birch, though there is not a bolder boy living.

Louisa being a pretty good judge of physiognomy, perceived instantly in the countenance of the Gentleman what his feelings were, and instantly retired in pursuit of a rod. When she returned the Gentleman took the rod from her hand, while she was employed in unbuttoning the youth's trousers, which, in the conflict between them, fell off. And now the battle raged on all sides. — As soon as she had placed the youth on her lap, and had taken the rod from the Gentleman, nothing was heard but "whip him well, my dear Madam!" "Yes, yes, yes, yes, yes! I'll take care to whip him in such a manner that he shall long remember!" "Oh! Pray Miss Louisa, my dear Miss Louisa, pray forgive me! Pray let me down and I'll never do anything to offend you again: I won't, upon my honour!" Whip him soundly, cried the father: I never saw a Lady handle a rod so well in my life! "Yes, yes, yes, yes! I'll take care his backside shall remember me!" said the Lady, turning her head aside and giving the father such a bewitching look that penetrated him to the soul. "Oh, Papa! Papa!" roared the youth, "pray save me, and indeed I'll never be bold again!" No, Sir, said the Lady, suspending the rod, and settling him on her lap, your Papa has delivered you into my hands now, and you'll find I'll teach you better manners! Will you ever trample on my flowers again? O that I were your step-mother! upon my honour your backside should be well acquainted with a rod before a week's end! Yes, yes, yes, you audacious urchin! "Oh, for God's sake, Miss Louisa, don't whip me any more! I promise you I'll be an excellent boy, and do everything you would have me! Indeed, indeed, I'll never disoblige you again! My Papa will be bound for me, I'm sure." Your Papa says no such thing; he says you are an ungovernable boy, and has begged me to whip you well, which I am determined to do before you get from under my hands! Oh, Papa, Papa, Papa! indeed I'll never do it again, upon my honour I will not, only intercede for me this once, and I'll love you while I live! "No, Sir," said the father; "the Lady knows when to have done; you have got into the hands you should have been in long ago, if I had been fortunate enough to have met with her, and I assure you she shall have the sole care of you in a few days! Whip him well, my dear, good Lady, he wanted such a woman to curb him!" Yes, yes, yes, yes! I'll curb him, I am resolved. Here she let him slip off her lap, pretending she could not hold him, and, after chasing him about the room, she laid hands on him and begged the father would horse him, which he instantly did. Stoop down, my dear Sir, said the Lady, you are too tall, and bear him above my reach. He instantly bent himself low, and Louisa, who, as has been said before, was an excellent physiognomist, now put her judgment to the trial; in short, she had often heard of men fond of birch from the beautiful hand of a Lady, and she wished to put her judgment to trial and see whether he was one of the sort. While she was settling the boy on the back of his father, she took care to remove the skirts of his father's coat in such a manner that when he stooped she had his bum in a proper direction, if it was uncased, for the rod. She had hitherto whipt the boy very gently, but now she gave him three or four strokes of the rod that made him caper and plunge with all his might. This was what she wanted, for it gave her an opportunity of letting fall some strokes on the father's bum, which appeared to fall accidentally in the contention. When the gentleman received a few of these, and beheld the lovely object that let them fall, his blood boiled within him from head to foot, and by the time he had received about a dozen strokes he could hold out no longer, so holding the boy with one hand, he unbuttoned his nankeen breeches with the other, which being pretty large soon fell to his heels. The oddity of the circumstance made Louisa smile, but she was determined to be serious, and therefore took no notice, but tucked in his shirt under his waistcoat, and made her lecture serve both. The strokes that fell on the boy were light to what fell on the father, for her accidental stripes were of the heaviest kind, as she thought by that means to rivet his affections.

It would be my greatest pleasure, cried she, to be step-mother to such a mischievous urchin, I would take the rod in hand every hour of the day! Miss Louisa, Miss Louisa, Miss Louisa! my dear Miss Louisa, pray let me down! indeed, upon my honour, — O dear, O dear, O dear — for God's sake pardon me! — You may kick and plunge and roar as long as you like, but I am determined to leave something on your backside to remember me! Yes, you great bold boy (here three or four heavy strokes fell on the father's bum), who, feeling he had enough, cried out to the Lady, I think, Madam, he has had enough. Well, said the Lady, I will lay aside the rod, but as a farther punishment he shall be blindfolded instantly, with his hands tied behind him, and shall stand behind the screen half-an-hour.

This the father was highly tickled at, as it gave him an opportunity of buttoning his breeches unseen by the boy, who was hood-winked by the Lady before the father let him down. The Gentleman was so delighted with the frolic altogether, that in less than a fortnight he married the Lady, and settled a jointure of six hundred a year on her.

The youth, who is now upon the verge of manhood, has declared to a demirep of distinguished beauty, that from being habituated to the rod from the hand of so lovely a woman, he connects, like Rousseau, this pleasure with that in general estimation. He has farther declared the sight of Louisa in full dress, though now past forty, sets his blood boiling with sensuality in an instant, as there is a certain air majesty about her few women possess.

C. W. M., who, in a letter to the Publisher, offered five hundred a year for life to a fine woman who would superintend the education of his children, and who would be content to live entirely in the country, is informed the Publisher knows no such Lady.

F I N I S

A new Edition of the First Part of this Work is just published. Ladies or Gentlemen who may wish to have those Pamphlets together, with Fashionable Lectures, composed and delivered with Birch Discipline, and Dr. Meibomius on whipping, bound in one Volume, may depend on having their Orders executed with punctuality.

N.B. — Orders or Letters of Information will be thankfully received by the Publisher.

Appendix

Bibliographic details from Pisanus Fraxi [Henry Spencer Ashbee], *Index Librorum Prohibitorum*: *Being Notes Bio- Biblio- Icono- graphical and Critical, on Curious and Uncommon Books* (London: 1877, pp. 238-249). The relevant page numbers of Ashbee's work are printed in bold, appear in square brackets, and are left aligned. Paragraph layout has been modified.

[**238**]

Exhibition of female flagellants, in the Modest & Incontinent World, Proving from indubitable Facts that a number of Ladies take a secret Pleasure in whipping their own, and Children comitted (sic) to their care, and that their Passion for exercising and feeling the Pleasure of a Birch-Rod, from Objects of their Choice of both Sexes, is to the full as Predominant as that of Mankind. Now First Published, from Authentic Anecdotes, French & English, found in a Lady's Cabinet. Embellished with six beautiful Quarto Prints, Superior to any thing of the kind ever Published. London. Printed for G. PEACOCK N°. 66. Drury Lane.

8vo; pp. 51; the title page is engraved, and the letters are mostly in italics; there is a pretty oval vignette representing

[239]

Cupid bound to a tree, and a young girl seated, preparing a birch to chastise him.* The work as it stands is complete in itself, although a second part was afterwards published.†

In 1872 J. C. Hotten reprinted this vol. (in 8vo., pp. 67, adding date 1777, and omitting any mention of the "plates,"‡ the title in other respects *printed* verbatim) and six other works on Flagellation, to be specified anon, which he classified as: " Library Illustrative of Social Progress. From the Original Editions collected by the late Henry Thomas Buckle, Author of 'A History of Civilization in England.' " He further had printed on separate sheets, and distributed among his *private* customers, the following circular and list:

" THE MANIA FOR FLOGGING AND THE BIRCH. "

" It is well known that the the late Henry Thomas Buckle, author of 'A History of Civilization,' collected a large library of curious books. Amongst the many topics that engaged his attention was the subject of CHASTISEMENT, viz., Discipline with a Birch or other implement. By rare good fortune, he collected an almost complete set of the astounding books issued by George Peacock, in the last century, and as no other examples of some of these rarities are known to exist, it is proposed to privately print a few copies as 'Curiosities of

---

* I have only seen one copy of this tract, which had been much cut down by the binder, it is probable that the title began with " The, " and there may have been a date. The copy in question was unfortunately *without* plates.

† See post, p. 245.

‡ This remark applies to the whole series, given on next page.

[**240**]

Literature.' Apart from their extreme rarity, the works are remarkable for the light they throw upon the state of society in the last century, and the mania that possessed all classes for chastising and being chastised.

"Accompanying this is a list of the 7 volumes already proposed. The price will be 15s. per volume, or £5 for the series, payable in advance. A volume will be issued each month, commencing with January 1872.

" The paper will be made expressly, and ribbed or wire-laid, precisely as the paper of the last century. The printing will be of the very choicest description; in fact, neither expense nor pains will be spared in the production.

" Should collectors of curious books care to pursue Mr. Buckle's studies farther, it is proposed to continue with the ' DANCING ' and other MANIAS that have in other times possessed society.*

" 1. EXHIBITION OF FEMALE FLAGELLANTS in the Modest and Incontinent World.

" 2. Part Second of the EXHIBITION OF FEMALE FLAGELLANTS in the Modest and Incontinent World.

" 3. LADY BUMTICKLER'S REVELS. A Comic Opera, as Performed at a Private Theatre with unbounded Applause.

" 4. A TREATISE OF THE USE OF FLOGGING IN VENEREAL AFFAIRS. Also in the Office of the Loins and Reins. By Meibomius.

---

* No other series except that at present under notice was done.

[**241**]

" 5. MADAM BIRCHINI'S DANCE. A Modern Tale, with Original Anecdotes collected in Fashionable Circles. By Lady Termagant Flaybum.

" 6. SUBLIME OF FLAGELLATION : in Letters from Lady Termagant Flaybum to Lady Harriet Tickletail.

" 7. FASHIONABLE LECTURES : Composed and Delivered with Birch Discipline, by the following Beautiful Ladies. "

Now in all this there is not a word of truth; the original tracts did not come from the library of Buckle, nor had he, in all probability, ever seen them. All seven had been for many years, and are still, in the possession of a well known London collector. They are bound together in one volume half calf, and in exactly the order in which Hotten reproduced them, but which is certainly not in accordance with the dates of their original publication. The fact is the present possessor of the volume in question lent it to Hotten, who had it surreptitiously reprinted, without the owner's permission or knowledge.

Hotten's edition consists of 250 copies of each vol., not more than 30 of which had been sold at the time of his death, the remainder of the issue was then disposed of in 1873, to Mr. J. W. Bouton, of New York.

Two remarks may at once be made concerning the whole series (excluding of course the able work of Meibomius, No. 4 of Hotten's reissue, which should not be associated with the other rubbish). In a literary point of view they are generally worthless, and are insufferably dull and tedious,—one

[242]

idea—one only—is harped upon throughout all of them, and this is not true to nature. Flagellation, if it has any value, is a preparation for, an incentive to, a higher pleasure (for it can scarcely be called a pleasure itself), a means towards an end, not the end itself. Now, in no single anecdote throughout the series is the flagellation immediately followed by anything else; the chastisement begins and ends each performance.

Further, it is always the woman who wields the rod, never the man, and this, to say the least of it, is entirely one sided; for there can be no doubt that men have as strong a predilection for whipping girls (and even boys) as for being whipped themselves.

With regard to the volume under consideration, " Exhibition of Female Flagellants " it is a collection of anecdotes in prose, illustrative of the passion for the birch when administered by the woman to the man; and in birching, as in most other things, skill and delicacy are necessary: " Know then thou silly girl, (said Flirtilla) there is a manner in handling this sceptre of felicity, that few ladies are happy in: it is not the impassioned and aukward brandish of a vulgar female that can charm, but the deliberate and elegant manner of a woman of rank and fashion, who displays all that dignity in every action, even to the flirting of her fan, that leaves an indelible wound. What a difference between high and low-life in this particular! To see a vulgar woman when provoked by her children, seize them as a tyger would a lamb, rudely expose their posteriors, and

[243]

correct them with an open hand, or a rod more like a broom than a neat collection of twigs elegantly tied together; while a well-bred lady, coolly and deliberately brings her child or pupil to task, and when in error, so as to deserve punishment, commands the incorrigible Miss to bring her the rod, go on her knees, and beg with uplifted hands an excellent whipping; which ceremony gone through, she commands her to lye across her lap, or to mount on her maid's shoulders, and then with the loveliest hands imaginable removes every impediment from the whimpering lady's b—e, who all the time, with tears, and intreaties of the sweetest kind implores her dear mother or governess, to pardon her; all which the lovely disciplinarian listens to with the utmost delight, running over with rapture at the same time those white, angelic orbs, that in a few minutes she crimsons as deep as the finest rose, with a well-exercised and elegantly-handled rod! " (p. 4). Compare with this a passage at p. 181 of " The Merry Order of St. Bridget, " in which the same idea is reproduced, and which I transcribe under that title.

Of the " Exhibition of Female Flagellants " there are two other editions, viz.:

" **Exhibition of female flagellants** Suus cuique mos. London : Printed at the Expense of THERESA BERKLEY, for the Benefit of Mary Wilson, by JOHN SUDBURY, 252, High Holborn. "

On this title page there is a vignette of a hand brandishing a

[**244**]

rod. A second title page, decorated with a small Roman lamp, gives us:

" **Exhibitio flagellantium.**

> Delicias pariunt Veneri crudelìa flagra ;
> Dum nocet, ille juvat, dum juvat, ecce nocet

Londini : Apud NOURSE et WINGRAVE. 1793."

Tall 12mo. (counts 6); pp. 58 including one title page only; 4 coloured folding plates of fair execution, and a well engraved frontispiece,* representing a very pretty girl wielding a birch, under which is the name " Mary Wilson." This edition, which was published about 1830, by JOHN CANNON, contains the same matter as the original, plus an " Advertisement, " signed THERESA BERKELY, in which is given a short account of MARY WILSON, and in which the first edition is mentioned as " originally published about fifty years since, and is now become so very scarce as seldom to be obtained, and then not under Five Guineas a copy."

The other edition is in the well known Holywell Street form, 8vo, pp. 64 in all, with 8 badly done lithographs; the title is identical with the English one of the edition immediately above mentioned, minus " John Sudbury, 252, High Holborn; " it contains all the matter in the original, the " Advertisement " mentioned above, and an addition entitled " Fragmenta " (p. 55 to end of vol.), which comprises an anecdote from " The

---

* Reproduced by Hotten as Frontispiece to his publication, " The Romance of Chastisement, " see that title.

[245]

Cherub, " * and one or two other anecdotes of the same class. This reprint was done about 1860, by W. DUGDALE.

" 𝔓art the 𝔖econd. of the 𝔈xhibition of female flagellants. In the Modest and Incontinent World. Proving from Indubitable Facts, That a Number of Ladies take a Secret Pleasure, In Whipping their own, And Children committed to their care; and that their Passion for Exercising and Feeling the exquisite Pleasure of a Birch-Rod, from objects of their Choice, of Both Sexes, is to the full as Predominant, as that of Mankind. Now First Published from a Lady's Manuscript, and a Number of Letters sent to the Editor of the First Part of this original Work. Embellished with Six highly-finished Prints, from beautiful Paintings. Price One Guinea Plain, or a Guinea and a Half in Colours. London: Printed for GEORGE PEACOCK, No. 66, Drury-Lane. MDCCLXXXV."

8vo.; pp. viii and 60; letter-press title. Reproduced by HOTTEN as No. 2 of the " Library Illustrative of Social Progress,"† 8vo.; pp. 84; from the title however is omitted the paragraph referring to the illustrations and price; further Mr. Hotten cut out of the " Preliminary Address " two passages in which prints are mentioned, and suppressed in toto a curious and facetious letter (covering, in the original, four pages), in which a correspondent, " PHILOPODEX, " communicates to the editor his

---

* Given in this work, see p. 159.
† See p. 240, ante.

[**246**]

opinions and advice respecting illustrations for "a very superb work to be forthcoming very soon, entitled, ' An Exhibition of Female Flagellants.' " " In the first place then, (he observes) I hope (a hope the title seems to encourage me in,) it will consist of a display of *Female* Backsides, for though I think a Ladies Bum uncovered an agreeable and diverting object, I would not give a farthing to see a man's A—, this I believe is only agreeable to persons of a certain description, too bad to be countenanced: But to see the representation of an agreeable young Lady having her petticoats pulled up, and her pretty pouting Backside laid bare, and seeming to feel the tingling stripes of a rod, is amusing enough: such is that excellent print of yours, the Countess Du Barre's Whim, which is nearly perfect in its kind—I would therefore, have your book contain such subjects and such descriptions—Now a word or two to the engraver. Let him pourtray the Lady's Backside, which no doubt will be the principal figure in the piece, round, plump, and large; rather over than under the size, which the usual proportion of painters and statuaries would allow; let him in general present it full and completely bared to the eye; though in some plates for variety, he may give it us sideling, or a little bit of the Ladies under petticoat or shift, shading some part of it, and, let it be remembered, that if he has that complete knowledge of his subject I imagine he has, and is a man of genius, a large field is open before him to display it in. He may show us several different sorts of Backsides, all of them natural,

[247]

and proper; all of them elegant and handsome (for there is almost as much difference in tails as in heads) but not all alike; he certainly will not give the little round firm backside of fifteen to five and thirty, nor the full mellow bum of the middle aged Lady, to the boarding school Miss." Philopodex proceeds to give directions as to the implement to be used, not " a great wisp of something which they suppose will do to represent a rod, " but a " stinging tickle-tail, the dread of naughty Miss—a tingling rod, which the admirers of this diversion might know to be made of their darling birch," and he hints: " It is probable that in some of these prints, there will be other figures besides the principal, the bare a—'d Lady; now though we cannot have the satisfaction of seeing the pretty bums of them all, an ingenious delineator might so contrive it, to heighten the lusciousness of the whole piece, that one by some careless posture might show her legs, another her breasts, and the dress of others might be so managed, as to give us the idea of a very large and full backside, concealed under the swelling drapery. Thus would each plate present us with a very beautiful and entertaining *tout ensemble*, and these little circumstances and adjuncts prove a seasonable relief to the eye, fatigued and overpowered by the blaze of beauty, from the naked a—e of the Lady enjoying the sweets of the Birch, darting full upon us, without the least bit of petticoat, or smock interposing, by way of cloud, to ease our scorched senses." "Philopodex" concludes in a " P.S. I thought it unnecessary to advise you, that

[248]

all the figures should be dressed; every Lady should have her shift on at least; nakedness must always in these matters be partial, to give the highest degree of satisfaction."*

The second part of the " Exhibition of Female Flagellants " is similar to the first—a collection of anecdotes about birchings administered by *female* hands; the use of flowers† in " re Veneria " is dilated upon: " After she had done (whipping her) she took Miss N. to the garden, and picked for her a beautiful nosegay, but so monstrously large that she was almost ashamed to wear it. However as her friend wore one of an equal size, she pinned it to her bosom; I see, my dear, said she, you are not acquainted with the secret influence of flowers; know my dear girl that their sweet perfume has an uncommon effect on many men and women; but to have that effect on men they must adorn a lovely bosom like yours." (p. 3).

According to the correct fashion the bouquet should be very large, and worn on the left side of the breast.

---

* Some other passages relating to illustrations, but of no material importance, have been expunged in Hotten's reprint.

† Refer on this subject to Mr. J. Davenport's " Aphrodisiacs and Anti-aphrodisiacs " (p. 107), in which he quotes Cabanis to the following effect: " Odours act powerfully upon the nervous system, they prepare it for all the pleasurable sensations, they communicate to it that slight disturbance or commotion which appears as if inseparable from emotions of delight, all which may be accounted for by their exercising a special action upon those organs whence originate the most rapturous pleasures of which our nature is susceptible. In infancy its influence is almost nothing, in old age it is weak, its true epoch being that of youth, that of love. "

[249]

There is yet another modern edition of the work, the title slightly altered:

" 𝔓art 𝔱𝔥𝔢 𝔖𝔢𝔠𝔬𝔫𝔡. 𝔗𝔥𝔢 𝔉𝔢𝔪𝔞𝔩𝔢 𝔉𝔩𝔞𝔤𝔢𝔩𝔩𝔞𝔫𝔱𝔰 𝔦𝔫 𝔱𝔥𝔢 𝔅𝔢𝔞𝔲-𝔐𝔬𝔫𝔡𝔢 𝔞𝔫𝔡 𝔱𝔥𝔢 𝔇𝔢𝔪𝔦-𝔐𝔬𝔫𝔡𝔢 ; proving from indubitable facts that the Secret Pleasure of Whipping their own children and those of others, and that the Delights of the Birch Rod are as powerful in the female as in the masculine part of humanity. Now First Published from the Manuscript of a Lady, and from Original Correspondence addressed to the Editor of the First Part. With highly Coloured Engravings. Two Guineas."

8vo.; pp. 62; 8 plates in all, fairly drawn and coloured, the frontispiece is a fancy design, a winged arse in clouds, encircled by male and female pudenda, with the words " Anecdotes of Female Flagellants. " This edition, which was published by W. DUGDALE in 1866, contains the whole of the matter in the original, including the letter of " Philopodex."

BIRCHGROVE PRESS
Flagellant & Libertine Erotica

Birchgrove Press specializes in producing new print and e-book editions of pre-1950s writings on sexual flagellation in English. Original editions of many of the books that we offer are difficult to obtain and are highly sought after. We are especially proud to offer new editions of rare Victorian flagellant texts such as *The Mysteries of Verbena House*, *Experimental Lecture by Colonel Spanker*, and *The Quintessence of Birch Discipline*. Birchgrove Press also produces new editions of libertine literature. We have published *Venus in the Cloister*, *The School of Venus*, *The Dialogues of Luisa Sigea*, and Isidore Liseux's translation of the Marquis de Sade's *Justine* (1791), *Opus Sadicum*, for example. For a full list of titles and formats, please visit our website:

www.birchgrovepress.com.